MY WORST IDEAS

Michael Jeffrey Lee

SPURL EDITIONS

Copyright © 2023 Michael Jeffrey Lee

Cover photograph "Sawmill at the Greensboro Lumber Co., Greensboro, Ga." (1941), attributed to Jack Delano, Farm Security Administration Collection

Author photograph by Erika Pellicci

Stories from this collection previously appeared in N+1, The Southern Review, The Rupture, Quarterly West, Columbia Journal, Parcel, Fairy Tale Review, xo Orpheus: Fifty New Myths, and Gigantic.

This is a work of fiction. Names, characters, places, and incidents either are the product of the author's imagination or are used fictitiously. Any resemblance to actual persons, living or dead, events, or locales is entirely coincidental.

Published by Spurl Editions

ISBN: 978-1-943679-18-8

Spurl Editions
www.spurleditions.com
spurlcontact@gmail.com

MY WORST IDEAS 5

THE YOUNG MAN WHO WANTED TO MAKE FRIENDS 9

THE BURNED-OUT HOUSE 13

FAMOUSTOWN 19

THE POOR MAN AND THE SANDWICH 33

THE SHIVERS 37

BABY LIGHT 49

BACK TO BLANDON 51

THE MOUTH 61

FIRST GHOST STORY 67

JUMBLES 69

I LEAD A PLEASANT LIFE 77

HEARD FROM WEST 87

OLD MOISTON 99

THE NIGHT YOU DIED 111

MICKEY'S PRAYER 117

MY WORST IDEAS 2 121

THE RIDDLER 127

MY WORST IDEAS

I have ideas for stories all the time: I might be standing on a bridge, looking down at the freezing water; I might be walking home late at night, trying not to be murdered; or I might be getting intimate with a significant other; but no matter where I am or who I'm with, my mind is working overtime, helping me generate fresh ideas and inspirations for my fiction – that's why I always keep a pen at the ready. There are days when I can barely jot my ideas down fast enough, and I can fill whole Moleskines without coming up for air – it's on those days that I feel my most healthy and human.

But some of my ideas over the years have been very bad – a few of them have made me downright ashamed of my own brain. Even worse are the bad ideas I insist on laboring over for long periods, bringing them all the way to draft form. A few years ago, I spent several months writing a story about an incarcerated man. He had done something awful, his execution day was quickly approaching, and the stress was causing him to lose his grip on reality: alone in his dark cell, he would hallucinate and see people who weren't really there, talking and dancing and carrying on with them until the wee hours. Then, the night before the state was set to murder him, something unexpected happened: he died in his sleep, an apparent heart attack. The story took a turn for the humorous, and the bumbling guards, fearful of legal action, tried to carry out the execution as planned, and spent the rest of the day attempting to fool the sheriff and the chaplain and the victims' family into thinking that the condemned man was still alive, right up to the point that the switch was flipped. I am particularly proud of the last supper scene, messy as it is, though I don't think much else about the story works – I realize now that the idea was just not original enough. Many authors have written that story better, and I had no business thinking I had anything new to bring to the table.

And just a few months ago, I found myself working on another dud – it was a story about a woman who dreamed every night about owning a hybrid car. She wanted to use less gas and help the environment, and even though such a car was well beyond her means it didn't stop her from thinking about it night and day. She was obsessed, and who could blame her? Also, she was very old, which I was hoping would make her more sympathetic. But then an interesting opportunity came her way: a famous game show began filming in her town, and something told her to try and get on it, so she did, and, just her luck, the grand prize of the day was a hybrid car, and through a combination of chance and skill she managed to win it. She drove it home that day – the happiest day of her life. But that's where her luck ended. She crashed the car the very next day, and before long, everything in her life was going wrong, and soon she found herself on the street. The last scene was quite ironic: a jeweled hand passing a single dollar bill out the window of a hybrid car to the protagonist, who stood shivering on a median beneath a freeway overpass. I didn't really like the story when I began it, and I *really* didn't like it when I finished it, especially because it seemed to imply that the old woman deserved a severe punishment for desiring something well beyond her means. I'm glad I lost the story when my computer got wet.

Just the other day I had another bad idea; from sunup to sundown I worked on this story that will probably never see the light of day. It was a tale of two roommates. They were friends, living in an apartment together. They were both working odd jobs and, interestingly, they were both involved in romantic relationships that were eating their souls. Anyway, one night, one of the roommates finally snapped, and he packed up his car and drove to the river and then drove his car into the river, but he decided at the last minute that he wanted to live, so he rolled down the window and escaped. The next day he cut ties with his sweetheart, purchased a bike, and turned his life around. The other roommate was happy for him but still mired in his own toxic relationship, which he persisted in for a few more weeks. Actually, I'm not really sure if this is a bad story or not. I know these people, and I feel too close to the material to be able to judge it accurately. But I suspect that it's bad, very bad and nasty and quite possibly my worst, and I don't think I'll return to it anytime soon.

Anyway, those are some bad story ideas, and if I wasn't so excited about the one I'm working on today – it's about a church group building toilets for some grateful villagers – I'd feel much more depressed about how much of my life I've spent working on them.

THE YOUNG MAN WHO WANTED TO MAKE FRIENDS

There was a young man who moved to a new town and couldn't make any friends. All the friends were taken, it seemed, and he found himself alone every day and night. One day, he was in the square, sitting on a crooked bench and eating his lunch. Potential friends were passing to and fro with each other, not even giving him a glance.

"If only I could make a friend," said the young man. "Then life would be bearable."

Just then a pigeon flew down and alighted next to him. "I heard what you said," said the pigeon. "I have a lot of pity for you."

"Thank you," said the young man, who had been looking for pity. "But will you be my friend?"

"No," said the pigeon, "but I will help you."

"You're very kind," said the young man. "I've had no luck here in this town."

"First," said the pigeon, "hold me in your fist nice and tight, and with a firm grip. Then with your other hand twist my little head off, quick."

"Fine," said the young man. "What then?"

"Toss my head in your mouth and swallow it whole, no chewing."

"Fine," said the young man. "And then?"

"Lift my body to your lips," said the pigeon, "and drink my blood in a single draft."

"And then?" said the young man.

"After every last drop is gone," said the pigeon, "put my headless corpse in your pants pocket."

"Easy," said the young man. "But how will it help me?"

"You will keep me in your pocket when you go around town. When you come close to a friend, I will heat my body up. Your pocket will get hot, and it will be a signal to you that you should engage them."

"Have you come from God?" said the young man.

"I've come on behalf of the mayor," said the pigeon.

"The mayor," wondered the young man.

"He has eyes in the sky," said the pigeon.

"And he would sacrifice one of his pigeons for me?" said the young man.

"It means that much to him," said the pigeon.

"Thanks to you both," said the young man. "Are you ready?"

"I am," said the bird.

So the young man seized the bird, twisted off the little head, popped it in his mouth, drained the body to the last drop and then put it in his pocket for safekeeping. As soon as he left the crooked bench and began walking around town, he could feel his pocket getting hotter. Hotter and hotter did it grow, until he came upon his first friend. He introduced himself, and they spoke for a little while, and then they made some plans. It thrilled his heart to have made a friend, and he set out to find more. Day after day the young man walked around town, making friends and making plans, with that bird nearly burning a hole in his pocket!

Time went by, and soon the young man was quite well-known in town, and there wasn't a single day or night that he did not speak with a friend. Policemen, office girls, homeless people, people from all walks of life – soon he was friends with so many. And the pigeon's body never decayed, nor did it fail him. Always it was in his pocket, heating up when he neared a potential friend, or cooling off around someone he needn't bother with.

One day, when he had made all the friends he needed to make, the young man set out to find the mayor, who lived on the outskirts of town, in a big house several stories tall, to thank him. But when he arrived at the mayor's house, weird things immediately started happening. On the first floor he saw a row of young men's skulls, grinning at him. They directed him one flight up. On the second floor he saw a bunch of young men's hands, waving at him. They too directed him one flight up. And on the third floor he saw a pile of smoldering private parts, and they too directed him one flight up. When he got to the fourth floor, he peered through the keyhole and saw the mayor sitting in his chair.

"He looks like a bird," thought the young man, but when the young man opened the door the mayor leapt out of the chair and into his bed, and pulled the covers all the way over his head.

"Mr. Mayor," said the young man. "What is all of this?"

"What are you talking about?" said the mayor.

"Weird things in your house," said the young man. "On the first floor, I saw a row of young men's skulls grinning at me."

"You poor child," said the mayor, "those were juicy melons ready to be eaten."

"And on the second floor," said the young man, "I saw a bunch of young men's hands, waving at me."

"You poor child," said the mayor, "those were spicy red peppers, flopping in the wind."

"And on the third floor," said the young man, "I saw a pile of smoldering private parts, and they too directed me one flight up."

"You poor child," said the mayor, "those were moldy carrot skins, waiting for the garbage can."

"And on the fourth floor I peered through the keyhole," said the young man, "and I saw you, Mr. Mayor, and you looked just like a bird."

At that moment the skulls, the hands, and the private parts came into the room and began to dance, and beneath the covers the mayor seemed to dance as well. The young man did what any other young man would have done in that situation: he took that hot headless pigeon out of his pocket, dropped it on the floor, and started to dance!

THE BURNED-OUT HOUSE

I was about 35 when I moved into the burned-out house. The room was affordable, and I didn't even mind the smell. I spread out my things, and it quickly felt like home.

I got a job as a hamburger vendor and started pushing a cart downtown. I'd purchase all the patties and buns in the morning, at the company warehouse, and then it was my job to sell them. After a good shift, I'd push the empty cart back home, a little damp cash in my pants.

I did all my shopping up the road, at this blasted convenience store. They had everything I needed, and sometimes they even carried green things. They carried my brand of liquor too, and the toilet paper they sold smelled like wet flowers. I used to blow my nose a lot in the burned-out house – that's how I knew.

Freight trains used to pass nearby, and their horns were pretty damn loud. Some nights I'd wake up and think I'd fallen asleep on the tracks. I'd cry out, like a bleating baby, but then I'd remember where I really was – on the floor in the burned-out house – and I'd let out a chuckle. And soon I'd be on my side again, snoring.

On my days off, I'd walk to the river to swim. If I was alone, I'd take off my clothes and swim naked, but if there were people around, I'd just dunk my head. The hamburger char would slide right off me and make a weird shadow in the water.

I had a good buddy during that time, a fellow about my age. He called himself The Doctor, and he lived in a normal house up the road. We'd walk downtown together on my days off, and he'd tell me about his girl troubles. Occasionally he'd buy me a drink or take me to a strip club, but mostly it was just us walking and him talking. I always thought The Doctor was gay, but he denied it every time. Still, I kept it up.

There was a dentist around too, although I wouldn't have called him a friend. But he made house calls and sometimes treated me for free in the yard. I'd sit in an old broken chair, and he'd tilt my head back and make me say "Ah." He helped with this massive abscess I had one summer, which was lucky, even though his drill was only working at quarter speed.

For a while I had a bike – I had found it abandoned by the river. I rode it for several weeks, cruising through the different parts of town. Then one night, just for shits, I decided to sell it, but that was a big mistake. Some of my happiest times were spent on that bike, goddamn it.

Sometimes, when I was bored, I would count the blue tiles in the bathroom of the burned-out house. I spent hours and hours in there, just counting those tiles. There was no door, but if I heard someone coming I would cough as a courtesy, or fart extra hard.

I did keep my drug abuse to a minimum when I lived in the burned-out house. Sure, once in a while, on the blackened table, I'd find traces of something my roommates had enjoyed, and I'd help myself, but otherwise I kept it pretty clean. I took a nasal decongestant every morning with my coffee, just to get my brain going, but that was about it.

I got a lot of reading done, especially on weekends. Old newspapers, cereal boxes – whatever was around. That honey-colored sunlight streaming in through the chinks in the walls always put me in a pleasant mood. If I'd had a television, I know I wouldn't have read as much. And if I'd had a computer? Forget it, I would've become addicted to hardcore porn.

I had a music collection during those years as well, a real luxury. A previous tenant had left a pile of tapes behind, full of random noises and voices, and I inherited them. Some mornings, after a really long night, it would bring me a lot of joy to permeate that burned-out house with sound.

Birds flew in and out of the house quite frequently, and sometimes they'd get badly harmed. One pigeon in particular, his wing got caught in the wire under the roof, and he died dangling. For months I would see him up there, swaying in the breeze and out of reach, and I used to wonder what it meant – that dead pigeon just dangling there in the burned-out house.

There was this skinny white dog that used to follow me in the streets whenever I was working. No matter where I was with the cart, he'd always be a block or two back, sitting on his haunches and watching me. One day I threw a patty down in the road, just to see if he'd come closer, but he stayed put. Then one day I saw that he'd been run over, the dumb mutt.

I made sure to shave regularly when I lived in the burned-out house, and I always tried to keep my nails and fingers neat. It would have been pretty shitty if a customer wound up with a curly beard hair in their bun or a dirty fingernail in their beef, and it also would have been my ass.

There was one romantic thing that happened to me. I bumped into a cute dairy vendor one day and we made a date. We got drunk by the river that night, then I walked her all the way home and had sex with her in her house before heading back. Later I ran into her again, and she told me that I'd gotten her pregnant, but she'd decided not to keep it. I asked her how come, and she said it was because she couldn't bear the thought of raising a child inside a burned-out house. "That makes two of us," I said, laughing so hard I almost choked.

I actually managed to quit smoking when I lived in the burned-out house, on The Doctor's recommendation. He told me if I wanted to keep drinking and living in a burned-out house, the smoking would have to go. I did what he said. I imagined myself living a nice

15

long life in those days, ha ha.

There was a joke I carried around in my head when I lived in the burned-out house, something along the lines of, "it smells so bad in this burned-out house that I'm starting to think that it's a burned outhouse." No one was home when it cropped up in my mind, so I kept it to myself, until now.

Things didn't always go so smoothly in the burned-out house. It was real close quarters in there, especially when everyone was home. One night I found a note on my yellow pillow from one of my roommates. He said he was going through a tough time and didn't appreciate me walking in on him when he needed to be alone. I wrote him back, telling him to stop using my notebook pages as toilet paper, but in the end I gave him his space.

I thought about carrying a gun on me when I lived in the burned-out house, but ultimately decided against it. Clumsy me, I worried I would shoot my foot or my dick off, so I settled for a simple blade. I carried it at all times and slept with it on my chest.

One of my roommates was determined to move out – that's all he talked about. He was a vendor same as me, but he wasn't blessed with the same sense of humor. One morning I saw that all of his stuff was gone, and I thought he'd accomplished his goal. But a few days later he was back in the burned-out house, spreading his rags out on the floor.

Some nights I thought that the burned-out house was just a state of mind – that, in fact, I wasn't really living in a burned-out house. I tended to think these thoughts on nights that were freezing, or when the wind was whipping ashes into my eyes.

I did lose a roommate for good, and that's a sad story. He wasn't a vendor, and frankly I don't know how he spent his days. He slipped on his way in one night and a big nail went right through his head. We buried him out back, near the previous tenants, and I marked the grave so no one would piss on it.

There was a very small church down the road, and sometimes I'd go to a Sunday service there. I'm not a believer, but I didn't mind doing the rituals. The people there were a different race than me, but they still let me sing and participate, which was generous. I think they could tell I was coming from a burned-out house, but they were always cool enough not to ask me about it.

I only spent one night away from the burned-out house. It was my birthday, and I'd booked myself a hotel room downtown. I drank several bottles of liquor and ordered some pizza delivery instead of eating the burgers I'd brought. Then I tried to sleep, but couldn't. I tossed and turned all night. Just as dawn broke, I had a brilliant idea: I left the room and crept back to the burned-out house. Within minutes, after jacking off, I was asleep.

Can a burned-out house catch fire again? I used to imagine that it could, usually at the end of my shift. I'd be pushing the cart around the final turn in the road, almost home, and I'd pretend I saw smoke, then fire, and then I'd hear myself say, "Oh, shit! She's going up!" But it would always be standing there, charred and cold, just as before.

When I was 39, I finally moved out of the burned-out house – I just gathered up all my things one day without warning and left. No one was around to see me off, as you might expect.

FAMOUSTOWN

The billboards started advertising the city long before I was even close to it. In fact, I'd barely left the Blandon City limits when I saw the following question floating in my periphery: WHAT DOES FAMOUSTOWN MEAN TO YOU?

Famoustown meant quite a lot to me, actually. Even though I'd never been there, it was a place I had been hearing about all my life. Big events were always taking place in Famoustown; it was a place that other places looked to for information on the current trends. It was also a place where famous people lived, and this had always given me pause. While I liked famous people just as much as the next person, I never wanted to be famous myself. After all, it didn't take much to see what fame did to people, how it puffed up their pride and let them speak every word with certainty; and how, over time, it seemed to make them resemble not the pleasant, ordinary people they surely were before fame found them, but rather mentally ill ghouls. And that wasn't going to be my route, I knew.

The problem was, the billboards just kept coming. Each time I saw one looming in the distance, I would squeeze my eyes shut until I knew I was well past it; and while this did help me avoid them in the short term, miles ahead, when my mind was blank again, they'd come roaring back, messages I thought I hadn't seen but in fact had, messages like, "WHERE WERE YOU WHEN YOU FIRST HEARD THE WORD FAMOUSTOWN?" or "IMAGINE A WORLD UNTO ITSELF UTTERLY UNTO ITSELF." And as I hurtled closer and closer toward the city, not even stopping to use the bathroom anymore but just urinating in the big-mouth bottles I

19

had saved, they grew harder and harder not to absorb, what with phrases like, "NO SUCH PLACE AS THIS" or "THIS PLACE RADIATES" or "IN PLACE OF THIS PLACE WHAT PLACE," and in fact these messages were so effective at catching my attention that I didn't even bother slotting them into my periphery anymore, instead cocking my head and letting them right into the middle of my eyes, messages like, "WHY WAIT FOR THE WORLD WHEN FAMOUS IS ALREADY FAMOUS" or "IF YOU DON'T VISIT IT MAKES NO DIFFERENCE TO US WE WILL REMAIN FAMOUS," and on and on, until I was just outside the city limits, and by that time, instead of dreading them I found that I was actually looking forward to them.

When I finally entered the city, the traffic announced itself all of a sudden, and I had to slam on my brakes to keep from causing an accident. The congestion was unlike anything I'd driven in before: in each lane, on either side of the highway, a line of vehicles stretching as far as my eyes could see, with bumpers that couldn't stop rubbing up against each other. I threw glances at my fellow travelers, hoping to show them a face that said WE ARE ALL IN THIS TOGETHER AREN'T WE, but the windows were tinted, and if the people did reach out to me, they did so from behind the black glass – more often than not, I was left looking at my own gaping face. Initially I felt a little hurt, but then I realized the vehicles might be full of famous people, famous people who wouldn't want, for any number of reasons, to be bothered by someone like me, and this made me feel a little better, almost excited to be sharing the highway with them.

Just then one particular billboard caught my eye. It depicted a very attractive woman, alone with an easel in a spacious room – she wore a fashionable hat and not much else – and she seemed to be deep within the artistic process. While her hand was busy applying paint to the canvas, her eyes, on the other hand, her eyes were peering very suggestively out at the viewer: me. In the right corner of the photo were the words, "RENTING NOW," and just beneath them a phone number. I found my phone and dialed the number: 1-800-FAM-TOWN. A pleasant, somewhat husky voice answered.

"Hello," it said. "Famoustown Lofts. What can I help you with?"

"Hello," I said. "I'm calling about the lofts." The sun was now pretty high in the sky, and I was starting to sweat.

"We have one left. Would you like it?"

"It depends. What is it like?"

"You saw the billboard, didn't you?"

"Yes, but they say the real thing is never like the billboard."

"In this case, it is," she said.

"So the loft is spacious?"

"Very. It also includes a balcony, which we couldn't fit onto the billboard."

"It sounds too good to be true."

"I should also tell you that it has a full kitchen, a nice shower, and central air."

"All of those are good things too," I said. "How much does it cost?"

I could hear her sigh a little. "Had you asked me when we first began leasing, you would have cried tears of joy. We were practically giving them away then."

"I'm sorry I didn't move to Famoustown sooner."

"It's for the best," she said. "The neighborhood has changed a lot."

"How so?"

"Back then, we couldn't keep our tenants long enough to fulfill their leases."

"How did they die?" I said, suddenly feeling less confident

about this loft.

"Our first wave was mostly artists, and they were targeted. You aren't an artist, are you?"

"Not at all," I said, and for the first time in my life I was thankful for the genes I'd been given. "I'm trying to get something started with my life."

"Good. You'll fit right in."

I looked up again at the billboard, and something truly did not add up. "If you don't want any artists living in your lofts, why would you feature a beautiful painter doing her thing on your billboard?"

Then I could hear her laugh, though in a faint, reticent way. "That's an old billboard. Initially, we did want artists renting here, knowing they'd pave the way for more sensible tenants. But times have changed. So, you like the woman on the billboard?"

"Very much," I said. "I like how ambitious she seems, but also how sensitive."

"That's very kind. The loft is yours if you want it."

"How much did you say it was?"

"Are you financially secure? I can't have you breaking your lease on me."

"I'm pretty secure," I said. My mother had saved for years, even skipped a few meals.

"Where are you right now?"

"On the highway, staring at your billboard."

"Okay, then take the Downtown Famoustown exit. Make a right onto Lumbar, and you'll run right into us. I'll be in my office."

"I look forward to meeting you. What kind of building am I looking for?"

"An old hotel. You'll see the LOFTS AVAILABLE banner if you squint."

Soon enough I made it to the exit, and finally down the ramp and onto Lumbar. I spied what looked to be an old hotel and was able to nab a spot right in front of it. After checking myself out in the mirror, just to make sure I didn't have anything foreign on my face, I stepped out.

On the sidewalk, young professionals of all shapes, sizes, and genders walked to work, dressed in handsome suits and carrying slender briefcases. I joined the throng, chuckling a little, because there I was, a young man in a brand-new place with all the time in the world, walking alongside professionals headed to their jobs – jobs they'd work, without break, for the rest of their lives. And I fit in so well, I knew, my suit just as swanky as theirs, that they would have never guessed that I was nothing like them, nothing at all, going not to my job but to my loft, about to sign a new lease on life.

The building was a little weather-beaten, and the façade could have used a few splashes of paint here and there – but I wasn't paying for any kind of exterior. By counting the small but cozy balconies stacked on top of one another, I was able to determine that the building was about forty stories high. I decided to ask, if given the choice, for a room about halfway up: I didn't want to be so high that I lost touch with what was happening on the ground – nor did I want to be so close to the ground that street noises were able to enter my dreams.

I went right in through the double doors and found myself in a long, somewhat dark lobby, with adjoining hallways that went this way and that. The air was very fragrant, but also full of allergens: I spent the first few minutes sneezing, coughing, and rubbing my eyes until they were red. The office was not labeled clearly, so it took me several tries, but I knew I had opened the right door when I saw an attractive older woman, decked out in stylish, somewhat funky clothes, seated behind a small desk. She smiled, and I smiled right back, and I could tell we were interested in each other. "You called about the room," she said.

"I did," I said. "Was it you who I talked to?"

"It was," she said. "Do I look anything like her?"

"Like who?" I said.

"The billboard girl," she said. "The woman painting the picture."

I had to catch myself from crying out, because they were one and the same person. "Yes, you do!" I said.

"But I look older, don't I?" she said. "You can tell me the truth."

"Only a little," I said, which was a lie – she looked quite a lot older. "But you're still attractive."

"Stop," she said.

"No, really," I said. "I've been driving all night, but you look really good to me."

"It takes work, you know."

"What does?"

"Staying attractive."

"I've heard," I said. "Thankfully, I'm still young and don't have to worry about that yet."

"You could be more attractive, if you wanted to be."

"I don't want to work at it," I said.

"That's okay," she said.

"I was a beautiful child," I said, though I'm not sure why I felt the need to tell her this.

"Your mother is deceased, isn't she?"

"She is," I said. "Very recently."

She stood up suddenly. "Would you like to see your room?"

"Yes I would," I said.

I watched as she – a little seductively, I thought – removed a long key from one of her desk drawers. "Follow me."

Inside the elevator, she pressed the button for the twenty-fifth floor, looked at me, and, after the doors had closed, began to cry. She didn't even try to be secretive about her tears; she just stood there and stared at me and cried. And because I was worn out from my drive, and because I'd never been able to contain my emotions around people who couldn't contain theirs, I started crying, just standing there and staring at her and crying, until about the fourteenth floor or so, when a young man and a young woman – both in suits – boarded the elevator together, and though they had their backs to us, I could tell by the way their shoulders shook that they too were crying. If you found yourself in that elevator alongside us and managed to keep your eyes dry enough to see the scene objectively, you might have mistaken the four of us for a family, a family that had just received the tragic news that the fifth member had died, and here we were on our way to view a body we were almost certain to identify.

When the elevator stopped at the twenty-fifth floor, the older woman and I both turned off our tears, squeezed past the couple, and stepped out. We found ourselves in a long oblong hallway, where photographs of dead famous people adorned the walls. "Why were you crying in there?" I said.

"On the ground floor," she said, "I was thinking about your dead mother, and how it must be difficult for a person so young to lose his mother."

"It's not too big a deal," I said. "And besides, it hasn't really hit me yet."

"And I was just about to stop, but then those two young professionals came aboard."

"Yeah, they made it tough."

"Oh, that wasn't it. Before those two, had you ever seen a young professional cry?"

I thought for a moment. "I don't think so."

25

"Young professionals never cry," she said, "because they're young, and they have their entire moneymaking lives before them."

"That makes sense."

"Their tears today can only mean one thing: the slump has finally reached Famoustown, and young professionals everywhere are going to have to bear the brunt."

"Are there a lot of young professionals in this building?"

"All my tenants are young professionals," she said. "Except you, of course. We don't know what you are yet."

We walked down the hallway, which zigzagged past many other lofts, lofts I would probably never see inside. As I caught myself staring longingly at one of the pictures on the wall, I said, "Do you think any of the famous people are going to have to bear some of the slump's brunt?"

"I certainly hope not."

"But fair is fair," I said. "The famous should share the load as much as the young professionals, I think."

"If the famous are forced to bear much of anything," she said, "this town will have to change its name. Is that what you want?"

"No, no, that's not what I'm saying," I said, but in my heart I was wishing that every famous person would be forced to bear a brunt so heavy that it shattered their ankles.

"Here we are," she said, inserting the key into a gray door.

The loft was just a barren white room, though it did feature all the amenities she'd mentioned. Seeing that the interior was up to my expectations, I hopped over to the sliding door and stepped onto the balcony, which was quite tiny – there was only room enough for my two feet, so long as I kept them close together – but there was plenty of vertical room, so I was able to stretch out my arms high above my head and feel the breeze on my hands. I had to be careful not to lean forward because of the low height of the railing, but I grinned just the same — now wasn't the time to start finding fault with a room I clearly loved.

All of Famoustown stretched out below me, and beyond that, the blue ocean. There were lots of sights to see below, all the brilliant architecture and technological marvels and whatnot, but something seemed so brittle and chintzy about it all that I couldn't bear to look for long; I was even tempted, for a moment, to spit on it.

Feeling comfortable with myself, even a little proud at how balanced I was being, I brought my hands down to my sides, leaned back against the sliding door, and closed my eyes. I daydreamed of two people making love in the ocean, deep beneath the waves. Neither had any eyes in their sockets, but that didn't seem to stop them from enjoying each other's company and private parts. It was a perverty little dream, I admit, but I knew it was nothing to be ashamed of — what lives inside the mind does so without our consent, and even with full consent the content can't always be controlled. I only felt bad about it when I discovered, after opening my eyes and gazing down, that there'd been an accident while I was out — someone had fallen from one of the balconies above me and met their death on the street below. Given the position of the sun at that moment, I knew that the dead person's shadow must have passed over me on its way down, and I was surprised I hadn't perceived the sudden change in light.

I returned inside and found, much to my surprise, that the room wasn't barren anymore. Instead, it was all set up for painting. My landlady stood at her easel in the center of the room, applying her brush to the canvas, and though I had only been gone for a moment she was already deep within the artistic process.

"You're an artist in real life?" I said, genuinely surprised.

"Aspiring. This space doubles as my studio."

"I thought this loft was available."

"Do you ever think about suicide?" she said.

"Not too much," I told her. "I try and stay positive."

"How inspiring."

"So, I inspire you?" I asked. I was fishing for a compliment, and really feeling the aftereffects of that sexy dream.

"Maybe," she said. "Or maybe it's the slump that's fired my imagination."

"What do you find inspiring about me?"

"There's something barely there about you. I like that. I can work with that."

Just to play hard to get, I picked up my suitcase and put on a leave-taking face. "Maybe it won't work out," I said. "I don't want to take your studio away from you."

"Maybe we can find a compromise," she said. "Do you plan on spending much time in the loft?"

"Yes, I think so."

"I mean inside the loft, as opposed to out on the balcony."

"Oh. No. I imagine I'll be out on the balcony quite a lot, except of course when I need to lie down."

"So it wouldn't bother you if I painted in here sometimes?"

"How often are we talking?" I asked.

"Whenever inspiration struck."

"I wouldn't mind," I said. "But I'm sure there'll be plenty of times when I'll need my privacy." Then I took a big risk, but she seemed to be warming to me, so I very silently took off my fancy shoes and my jacket, my pants and my underwear, and stood before her in nothing but my skin. Instead of focusing on my nubile body, she kept her eyes focused on the canvas.

"You don't strike me as a very private person," she said.

"I am," I said. "I'm actually quite private when I need to be." I started clapping my hands together, in the hopes of getting her attention. Finally, one of her eyes rolled away from the canvas and fell on me, but it quickly rolled back.

"I can respect your privacy," she said.

"Thank you," I said.

Then I lay myself down on the floor and started writhing back and forth. "I'm being pretty private right now," I said. "In case you hadn't noticed."

"We are not going to lie down," she said. "It wouldn't be right."

"Please? I would really appreciate it."

"I'm a married woman," she said, showing me her ring.

"Oh shoot, I'm really sorry," I said, getting up from the floor and dusting myself off. "Why didn't you tell me?" I stepped back into my clammy slacks. I didn't even bother with the underwear because they were so clammy that I couldn't even pull them over my legs.

"I forget sometimes," she said. "My husband's away so often."

"What does he do?"

"He's famous."

"Oh, wow," I said. I felt my heart begin to race.

"Wow is right. I only wish he made more time for me."

"So he's neglectful?"

"More distant than neglectful."

Right before putting my jacket back on, I decided to give it one more go. "Are you sure you don't want to lie down with me, even for a minute?"

"No, thank you," she said. "Besides, I'm almost done with my painting."

Realizing that there was no chance of intimacy, I seized the opportunity to talk a little business. "Seeing as we're about to share a space together," I said, "how would you feel about giving me a discount on the rent?"

"That sounds fair. But I need it up front, of course."

I reached into my pocket, but then remembered just how stuffed with money my wallet was, so I took it out only after turning my back.

"Will this do?" I said, holding a big bill over my head. "For the first month, at least?"

"It's more than enough. Would you like to see my work?"

"Yes," I said, and she turned the easel around. The painting was awfully abstract, but after a few minutes of looking, I could discern what was going on clearly enough: it depicted me, or someone that looked like me, on a balcony, in the nude, with the skyline and the blue sky beyond me. My arms were stretched over my head, but my palms were pressed flat against each other; it looked as though I was preparing to take some sort of high dive.

"It's beautiful," I said. "I wonder about my hands, though."

"What about them?"

"I wasn't holding them that way," I said.

"Oh, you were," she said, using a tone I did not appreciate.

"I don't think so. I was holding them straight up in the air, like this." I demonstrated the pose for her.

"You should keep believing that."

"Why?"

"I'd like to keep you around for a while," she said, sweetly.

It was then that my stomach reminded me of its existence, so I put on my leave-taking face again – this time I meant it. "I'm going to get something to eat," I said. My tone of voice suggested there wasn't going to be any argument about it.

"Would you like some company?"

"I think I need to be alone."

"My, what a big bug you are."

"What are you talking about?" I said.

"You," she said. "A big bug."

"Maybe," I said, smoothing out my suit.

"A big bug doing big things in the big city, all by himself."

"Sure," I said, playing along. "And maybe after this big bug puts something in his stomach, he's going to go on the hunt for a special someone."

"Oh, really? For what purpose?"

"To lie down with," I said. "Since other bugs aren't quite as willing."

"Is that so?" she said. "A special someone?"

"That's right," I said. "A special sort of someone, who might not yet know this big bug is out and looking around."

"They'll be lucky to meet you, big bug."

"I am a big bug, aren't I?"

"You've got money, you've got health. What else would you need?"

"I've got it all, except for some lucky someone."

"Some soon-to-be lucky someone."

"Right," I said. "Some soon-to-be lucky someone. Who knows? I might even meet my sweetheart out there."

"Out where? Where's a sweetheart?"

"Out there," I said, pointing outside. "Out there, in the fun."

"Out there in fun Famoustown?"

"Out there in fun Famoustown."

"Maybe some food, something to drink?"

"Food and drink, yes. I'm old enough to mix the two."

"Is that all? That can't be all."

"Food and drink and money and health and some lucky someone to lie down with in fun Famoustown tonight, all within a big bug's reach."

"Come here and give me that rent," she said. "Don't wait one second more."

"Coming." I put on my jacket, then my shoes, and then walked over to her and pushed the money into her hand.

"Now go out and do what you said you'd do."

"Here I go," I said, and I smiled at my landlady, who smiled back, insanely attractive even in her aged state. I hugged her, kissed her on her wrinkled but beautiful cheek, then left the loft.

THE POOR MAN AND THE SANDWICH

A man was eating a sandwich one day on a city sidewalk. He was very poor, and had just spent the money he had made begging on the sandwich he was now eating. He had been so hungry when he had sat down that he had not only forgotten to say his prayers, he had also forgotten to pace himself and eat slowly. Soon the sandwich was finished and the man sat on the warm sidewalk in the late afternoon sun, sandwich juices staining his already dirty clothes.

"I should have saved half for later," he thought to himself, letting the sandwich paper flutter away, "but isn't that just like me to do, blow through something quickly without thinking of the consequences. Oh well, I guess I'll go hungry tonight, that's nothing new. I'll bed down right here in my usual spot, and maybe I'll have a nice dream or two. And in the morning I'll beg again, and maybe make enough for another sandwich, and this time I won't be so hasty."

Such were the poor homeless man's thoughts as he sat there digesting his sandwich as evening came on. He stared at the pedestrians scurrying this way and that and at the vehicles streaming by in the street, but no one paid him a passing glance. "I can't say I blame them," said the poor man, shaking his head. Soon he grew sleepy, so he lay back on the sidewalk and almost immediately began to dream.

In the dream he was on the same street he was actually lying down on, but he was sitting up and he was begging. And he was not alone – a poor girl sat beside him, very dirty and with her hands held out to the passersby. Much to the man's dismay, the girl was having all the luck – coins were finding their way into her dirty hands, not his own. "I suppose that's to be expected," thought the poor man, who understood he was dreaming. "Children tug at the heartstrings more than the middle-aged. Only I hope she shares some of what she makes, so this can be a nice dream."

But the hours wore on and the girl did not share her earnings. Soon she had crossed the street and was gone. "Oh well," said the poor man. "No surprises there. But maybe I'll dream something else now, and it will be more pleasant."

No sooner had he said this than the scene began to change; very soon he was dreaming another dream. But once again he was seated on the very same street, and on the very same sidewalk, but now it was the middle of the night. And once again he was not alone – another poor man, also very dirty, lay dead next to him. He had a knife stuck in his chest.

"This is terrible," thought the poor man. "I didn't kill that man, but it would seem to almost any passerby that I did, and that wouldn't be good. I can see it now: I'll be arrested, put on trial, get convicted, and probably even be executed. This is really stressful. I hope I dream something else soon, and that it's much nicer."

Soon, just as he'd hoped, the scene began to change, and he was dreaming yet another dream. Just as before, he was on the same sidewalk and street, but now it was dawn, and the sun was pouring down its pure, beautiful light. The man was very hungry, but he was alone.

"This is much nicer," he said. "This is certainly more of what I had in mind."

No sooner had he said this than the street began to come alive. People left their homes and apartments and took to the streets with vim and vigor. "Ah, the start of a new day," said the poor man. "It makes me happy to see the world warm up like this. But there's something strange about these people, I think. Hmm . . . something funny seems to be going on . . . "

The man perceived the situation correctly. As the people drew closer, he could plainly see that the people were not really people at all. Or, rather, if they were people, they had the quality of having sandwiches where their heads should have been!

"Ha, ha," said the poor man. "It's not a nice dream, but it makes me laugh just the same. Maybe I'll eat some of these heads whole right now, and not save any for later. But no, that would be too gross. Oh, my, what a silly dream . . . what a silly, silly dream . . . "

This was the poor man's final dream of the evening. He awoke in the middle of the night with a horrible stomachache. "That sandwich gave me funny dreams," he said to the dark, empty street.

THE SHIVERS

It was Monday so the restaurant was closed. In two days it would be my birthday, but I'd be back to work then, so if I was going to have a wild night it had to be that night. I sent messages to a few people to see what they were doing, but they were all busy – they all had to work the next day. *What are you going to do?* I asked myself. *It's not late, just barely dinnertime.* I dug out a few twenties from my drawer and slipped them into my wallet. *I wonder what I'm going to do tonight*, I said to myself, walking down the stairs and getting astride my bike, *I wonder where this bike will lead me.* Well, the first place it led me was to a little dive bar down the street, and I had to flash my ID at the door to be admitted. I didn't want to drink – I had stopped drinking when I moved to town – but I did want to get some of the food they serve. I hadn't eaten all day and was starved. I gave a nod to the sexy bartender and went to the little window in the back and ordered the beef special. The cook there is a whiz with beef and when I have the money I never miss a single one of his creations. I twiddled the knobs on a video game while waiting for my food, and when I saw the cook bring it out, I walked to an empty table and sat down and he put the food down in front of me. He told me to enjoy myself and I smiled and said I would. I ate it quickly, burying my face in it and letting the juices run down. I didn't drink any water because I didn't want to bother the bartender. She knows I only come for the food and she can't make any money off me, and it makes her upset. On my way out I got a napkin to give my mouth a final wipe, and I thanked the cook for everything. He asked me what I had going on that night and I told him I didn't really know yet, although I was hoping something fun would come along. He told me it was still early, and he didn't see why it wouldn't. Then I left and got back on my bike, but I didn't get too far down the road before I remembered a prescription that needed picking up at the pharmacy, so I went and did that. I thought I had refilled it by phone but when I went to the window they said I hadn't, so I told them to go ahead. I wandered the aisles for a while, checking out some of the new products that had arrived. Some things called Vita-Jolts were on sale, and they looked interesting. I was running low on allergy tablets and considered getting some more, but I didn't want to eat too far into my allotted money for the night. I did manage to pick out a tasteful sympathy card for my aunt, whose son had just died. Soon I was carrying out a black bag containing my prescription, the sympathy card, and a bottle of water, and I shivered for a second. It had gotten weirdly chilly since I'd been inside. But I wasn't half as cold as the people waiting for the bus across the street – most of them didn't have any warm clothing on. For some, every day is like a wild night. A song my brother used to sing about poor people suddenly flashed through my mind, but only the chorus: *I love them, even if they're messy. I don't care, goodbye*. I sent my brother a message, telling him I just remembered his poor people song and asking how he was doing. While waiting for the reply, I decided to bike back home for a minute and drop off my loot, so I headed back that way, letting the bag swing freely from one of my handlebars. The cars on the road kept their distance, though they sped by really fast. I had a helmet but had loaned it to a friend who had lice and didn't tell me, and I kept forgetting to get the spray I needed. I got home without any issues, and knew it would be such a short visit I risked leaving my bike unattended, leaning it against the side of my building. As soon as I was upstairs I ripped the top off the medication and shook some pills out into my hand, then washed them down with the bottle of water. They were for my cold sores, which I thought I had beaten once and for all, but they had recently made a strong showing down below. It felt good to be fighting back a little. I put the medicine bottle in the drawer alongside my money and was about to head out but then remembered the sympathy card. I took it out of the bag and saw that some of the condensation from the water bottle had wrinkled the envelope, so I took the card out of the envelope and threw them both on my bed and turned the fan on them. I grabbed a jacket from my closet and headed to the bathroom to urinate quickly, and then I darted back down the stairs and out the door. My bike was still there, as I hoped it would be. I checked my phone to see if anyone had had a change of heart but none had yet, so I headed downtown. I had to watch out for potholes and pieces of debris in the road, but I didn't have any issues. I rode over to the square, but it was the usual batch of people: drug addicts, mostly, definitely not my type. I lingered for a few minutes at the edge, hoping to see that fortune teller that I like. She's very striking, with a look that could swallow a person whole, and she usually works Mondays. She's given me a few readings before – they have all been bad – but she wasn't there, so I kept on. I rode by some of the more expensive stores in town and did a little window-shopping as I rolled by. There was no traffic behind me, so it didn't matter. I wasn't sure where I was going next, although I felt myself pulled in the direction of the casino. I liked the casino fine but didn't really want to go there on my night off, at least not this early, because it doesn't tend to get wild until later. Wouldn't be bad as a plan B, I decided. But in the meantime I was on the lookout for other fun activities. There were bars on just about every corner and I could hear laughter coming from inside them – dark laughter. I like to have a good time just like anyone else, but there is a kind of laughter that you hear downtown in some of these bars that makes me think that it is not a person laughing at all but a skull without skin on it, laughing at the fact that it has no skin, and it gives me the shivers. Then something unexpected happened: I don't know if it was the food I had eaten or the medicine I had taken, or the fact that I had washed it all down with that enormous bottle of water, but I felt myself having to go. I've never minded squeezing in between two parked cars and letting it fly, but this wasn't that, this was going to take a little longer. Rather than risk it in one of these bars – you never know if the locks on the stalls are working – I decided to ride back home and do my business there. So I headed back that way and got there just in time, and some minutes later when I was back in my bedroom, taking another twenty from my drawer, I saw that the envelope had completely dried. I turned off the fan and raced back downstairs, hopped back on the bike, and sped off toward downtown again. My next stop was the casino – I had decided I wanted to go to the casino after all. It was still early and it would just be a starter. I was there in less than ten minutes and flashed my ID at the door, and the greeter noticed that it was only two days until my birthday, and she said she hoped I'd come back to celebrate. I told her that unfortunately I had to work on my birthday, so this was going to be my wild night for the week, if not for a while. She nodded and wished me luck in whatever game I chose to play. I thanked her and told her I liked her low-cut dress, and she gave me a coy smile. I decided on blackjack. I wandered over to the tables, going back and forth between a few before I found a good one. I wedged myself between two high rollers, and it was a good spot to be in. They coached me on certain hands, told me when to hit and when to stand. I drank an energy drink while sitting there, which was placed before me without my even ordering it, and it definitely helped increase my focus. There was a no-nonsense lady on the button too, and she didn't make one false move. She liked me, I think, even winking at me every time I won a hand. I battled up and down for about an hour – I went as high up as a hundred, and then as low as my last twenty, but finally leveled off at around eighty. Eighty dollars in pure profit. I decided to call it quits. I thanked everyone and told them good night, although I knew of course that my night was just beginning. Because my previous meal had gone right through me, I was suddenly hungry again, so I slipped real quick into the buffet area. I made a small plate for myself – garlic bread and French fries and a few nuts – and ate near the exit. I rode back home straightaway because I did not like the idea of traveling with those extra twenties in my pocket – they made me feel crazy. As wild as I wanted this night to be, I didn't have any business blowing money I needed for basic necessities. But on the way back I couldn't resist stopping for ice cream – it felt right, after my victory. I love ice cream and once the thought gets in my head and I see the scoops there's no stopping me. While seated in the parlor I took some pictures of myself licking the cone and then I sent them to my friends, and one wrote back and said that it looked like fun. I ate it quickly, taking big bites, and I caught a real buzz from the sugar. I got on the bike again and charged back down the street and made my house in almost record time. But there was a creepy person rooting around in my garbage can when I pulled up, so I decided to bring my bike inside, into the rat room. There's no light in the rat room – it's just the place where I store my bike. The rats live there; it's their kingdom, and as far as I know they've never come up to see about me. I raced up the stairs, then threw those four twenties I had just won – minus the ice cream and buffet money – into the drawer. I shook out a few more pills just to be on the safe side, swallowing them without water. Then before closing the drawer I took back one of the twenties and put it in my wallet, just in case. It wasn't going to be a crazy wild night, maybe, but I thought it wouldn't be a bad idea to travel with a little extra. I was in a hurry to leave, but my stomach started feeling a little rumbly again, so I put on water for tea. While waiting for it to boil I went and sat down on the toilet and read a magazine. There's no seat, but once the bowl warms up it can be a really comforting place. The magazine I read was actually just a catalogue called *Red Cello*, which has been sent to me every month ever since I broke my leg and shattered my pelvis a few years back, in another town. It was assisted living products, neck straighteners and armchair-wheelchair combos, and glasses that allowed you to lie flat in bed but be able to read a book on your chest. I was only able to force a few drops out of my penis, but still it felt like something. Then I heard the kettle screaming, so I went to the kitchen and dropped a tea bag into a mug and poured the boiling water over it. I watched the water turn brown, took a few sips, and carried it over to my bed and held the cup between my hands, sitting on the edge of the bed. The tea was already helping my stomach and I felt ready to head back out into the night. But when I was halfway downstairs I felt the need to double-check the burners, so I ran back up and checked, and sure enough, the right front one was still going, burning a little too close to the black bag I keep my oatmeal in. Still not knowing what my next stop was going to be, I ran back down the stairs and flung the door open, then rolled my bike out backward. That scary person was still rooting around in the can, making a real night of it, so I quickly locked the door and sped off. I riskily checked my phone while I was riding but no one had gotten in touch yet. My brother, I knew, would come through eventually, even if what he sent was just gibberish – we liked to communicate through gibberish, most of the time. My head was pretty empty as to options at this point, and so I found myself pedaling back toward the first bar I went to. There would probably be a band playing now – a loud band, more than likely – and the whole bar would be begging for them to blast their ears more and more with every song, to almost kill them with their volume. I flashed my ID at the door again and the bartender didn't even notice me this time. There wasn't a band playing, but it was a little more crowded than earlier. I even saw the fortune teller I like so much. She was sitting at the end of the bar, but she looked as though she was on a date and I decided not to bother her. I went back to the window again to say hello to the cook, but he wasn't around – there was a different cook there and I like his cooking a lot less. He asked if he could help me and I didn't exactly want to say that I had been looking for the first cook, so I examined the menu instead and told him I needed a minute. I realized that I hadn't eaten anything green in a while, so I ordered the pork salad. I was hoping to busy myself at the video game again, but there was someone already fiddling with the knobs. There was no place to stand and lean against the wall, either – spikes jutted out from almost every inch of the place. In fact, the only available seat was at the bar, right next to the fortune teller and her date. I sat next to her and she immediately turned the other way. The bartender put down an ice water for me and started walking away, but I waved her back and ordered another energy drink, and she brought that for me. I took out my phone again and wrote a little gibberish to my brother, and this time he wrote a little gibberish right back. We went back and forth for a few minutes and I felt happy, and then the pork salad was placed before me and I ate it. It must have been the smell of the dish that grabbed the fortune teller's attention, because she swiveled her stool around and asked me what it was. I'm always so nervous around her: she has the oddest bone structure, and long black hair like my mother used to have. I told her it was the pork salad and she nodded and swiveled back around. Just before leaving I decided to do something bold: I tapped her on the shoulder and asked her if she knew of any wild or fun things happening in town tonight, if she had heard about anything exciting going on. Her eyes were nearly shut and I realized just how intoxicated she was. She said there was supposed to be a party at the park, something commemorating the new slave statues. I asked if she was going there later and she shook her head. I thanked her for the information and went out to my bike and started biking toward Riverfront Park. I don't know why I hadn't thought of it earlier. I hang around there frequently when I'm not working. Usually it's just children and dogs and I've never known it to be a wild place, but I was more than ready to be surprised. I pedaled faster and faster just thinking about it, and I stupidly took a turn too fast. I leaned left too hard and the bike started to go down. I was able to break my fall with my hands, and I lost some skin to the road. My head took a rather big knock – other than that I was fine. I even laughed a little at all of it. *You're trying to have such a wild night*, I thought, *that you've gone and endangered your precious body, the one thing that's really your own in this world*. My head was bleeding a bit, enough to warrant some sort of attention, so I knew I had to duck back home for a minute to treat it. *Just for a minute*, I thought, and then I would check out the party. I hadn't danced in a while and thought that it would do me good. I was a little shaky on the bike for the first few minutes and was definitely extra jittery as the cars and tanker trucks blew by me, but I made it home just fine. The blood had more or less dried by the time my building was in sight. There was no person rooting in the can this time, but I still wanted to play it safe and bring my bike inside. As I was rolling the bike into the rat room I heard a voice say *shut up*, and then I felt cold steel at the back of my neck. My luck in this town had finally run out. I heard the door close and I was instructed to walk up the stairs. I asked the person what they wanted, but they just told me to shut up, shut up. Then when we were upstairs I was instructed to take down my pants and bend over my bed. I did what I was told, fearing for my life. While bent over I heard my drawer open, and I imagined my twenties being found, and the bottle of pills too. For some reason I worried about them being taken – I knew that the pharmacy wouldn't give me another refill for a month. Then I heard a small tearing sound, which, in hindsight, was the sound of my attacker finding an old condom at the bottom of the drawer and unwrapping it. The next thing I knew, I was being penetrated, and while it was happening, I fixed my eyes on the sympathy card I had bought for my aunt. My attacker had a very small penis – if it was in fact a penis – although it was still quite painful. It was over quickly, though: soon I was hearing my attacker tell me he would kill me if I ever said anything, then footsteps on the stairs; there was him banging around in the rat room and the sound of my bike rolling backward and then I heard nothing. I pulled up my pants and checked my phone, and I went to the stove and put on water for tea. I went and sat back down on the toilet for a while and read more of *Red Cello*, basically determined to get on with my night. I was bleeding a little from the anus, I noticed, so when I was finished on the toilet I disinfected both the cut on my head and the one down below. I wondered why my attacker had used protection – it's possible he had seen my cold sores. I'd always considered them a curse, but who knows? I sat on the edge of my bed, drinking tea and feeling sore, and then for some reason I decided to write the sympathy card to my aunt. I found a pen and put the card in my lap and very calmly wrote: *Hello, I was very sorry to hear about the death of your son. Suicide is maybe the saddest way to go and all it does is leave victims, so they say. If you ever want to text me or call me on the phone, here is my number. Don't be afraid to contact me, day or night. Yours Truly, Mickey Shane.* I read it over again and it sounded like a bunch of gibberish to me, and on top of that I hadn't even written my real name. I closed the card and licked the envelope and then found a stamp in my drawer and slapped it on. The attacker hadn't taken any of my money, nor had he taken any of my pills. I put all my twenties and my pills into my jacket pocket. I found my folding knife in the drawer too, and I put that in my pocket as well. Would it have come in handy earlier? Probably not. I put the sympathy card in my jacket pocket too, and I felt ready to go. But then I had a funny idea and I don't know why. I went over to my small closet and dug around for a minute, until I located what I wanted and pulled out a white bob wig that I wear sometimes on Halloween and other holidays. I put it on, then went to the bathroom mirror and fixed it just so. It was really transformative, and it would have taken someone that knew me really well to see that it was me under there. I was going to take a picture and send it to my friends but decided against it – they wouldn't understand. It felt good to have something covering my head, and I gingerly made my way down the stairs. It was a little bit of a relief that my attacker had taken my bike, because the thought of that seat grinding back and forth between my legs was making me feel a little sick to my stomach. I set out again on foot and started down the road. I got a lot of honks because of the wig and some trucks even pulled over, but I walked quickly, with a sense of purpose. I saw a mailbox and tossed the sympathy card in and kept walking. I found that my legs were carrying me back to the bar, but I knew that I wasn't hungry anymore. I decided that I wanted a drink of something. I flashed my ID at the door one more time and went straight to the bar with a strange new confidence, and I sat down hard on the stool and told the bartender that I wanted three whiskeys. She looked shocked but poured them out anyway and I gulped them down and I felt very focused. I took out a twenty from my jacket pocket and slid it across the bar and told her she could keep the change. On the street, I was extra alert to debris in the road and to potholes, and I didn't stumble once on my way to the square. I think my body knew what I was going to do before my mind did. I took a seat on a bench, leaving plenty of space for someone else to sit should they want to. I sent out a few last messages to my friends, telling them I was calling it a night. I even got a few replies, saying we should get together soon. Everything was going to be okay, and I really didn't have to wait long for the thing to happen. I sat there, running my fingers through my wig and taking deep breaths. Soon a horrible-looking man rode by on my bike – the red flecks on the frame gave it away. He circled the square a few times, probably looking for someone he recognized, and not seeing anyone, he slowed down and hopped off and brought the bike up alongside the bench and sat down next to me. He really had no idea who I was, even though, if he were paying attention, he would have seen that the jacket and the pants and the face were the very same. He made small talk with me about the niceness of the night, and then when I asked him what kind of night he'd had he said he'd had a wild one, and when he asked what kind of night I'd had I said I too had had a wild one, and then he admitted that sometimes he wondered if he could keep up these wild nights for much longer, and I said I felt the same, admitting that there were plenty of mornings when I wondered just how much longer my body could put up with these wild nights. I smiled beneath the bob, knowing it was time. I said, "Hey, look at the person doubled over on the steps," and he did, and in one swift motion I had the folding knife out and was sawing into his windpipe. Actually, I sawed for quite a while, and really made a huge mess. The square was dark and quiet, and the only person who had seen my deed was the fortune teller – she was staring at me from her seat at the table nearby. *It had to be done*, I said. *It had to be done*, she nodded. I got back on my bike, but the seat had been lowered significantly, so I had to stand. I started pedaling home, more than ready to call it a night.

BABY LIGHT

Baby Light visited me last night. Hanging, as was his wont, from the streetlight outside.

His friend Pie Face had died. That was the first thing he told me. He said that Pie Face had been killed. Murdered in his bed while he slept.

I asked him who had done it, but Baby Light did not know. There were no suspects. Then he said that the mayor was set to speak tomorrow, about crime.

That particular crime? I asked.

All crime, said Baby Light. He asked if I planned on going, and I told him I wasn't sure.

Then he asked if I had seen his friend L.J. pass by, but I hadn't. What about Miggy Concert, he wanted to know, had I seen Miggy Concert?

I said again that I hadn't.

He asked if I wanted to hear the story of his conception. I told him I wouldn't mind.

His mother was a greasy sheet, he said, and his father a torn kite. One night they'd lain together, and in the morning there was Baby Light.

I asked if he had any siblings, but he didn't want to talk about that.

I asked if he had anything else to report, and he said that he didn't.

BACK TO BLANDON

I received a very warm welcome when I returned home after my long trip abroad, warmer than I could have ever imagined. As my ship pulled in, a small crowd gathered right there on the dock, waving their hands and handkerchiefs, crying excitedly and smiling in my direction. I noticed one among them who neither waved, smiled, nor cried – so I made up my mind to say a few words in his ear once we were face-to-face, but as we floated closer and I was able to see the scene much more clearly, I discovered the reason for his rudeness: he was busy fishing. His hands were occupied with his rod, his eyes were fixed on the water, and he was murmuring something softly to himself. It wasn't that he was choosing to ignore me, it was just that he didn't immediately perceive me, and after realizing this, I relaxed again. I drew a deep breath in through my nose, exhaled through my mouth, and did my best to delete that mental note I had just made. Then I lifted my arms up into a wave, began a high cry in my throat, and turned the corners of my mouth up into a smile.

I didn't have any luggage with me, just the shirt on my back, my pants, and my shoes. I had started my journey home with a nice gray hat, but while passing over particularly deep waters a stiff wind had blown it right off my head and sent it skimming over the waves. The shirt I wore was quite colorful, but also full of snags and splits. It covered me in the right places, though. My pants were in much better shape – a family I'd stayed with abroad had given them to me, which was surprising, given how tattered their own were, and I almost didn't take them, but after reminding me of all the free literature I had given them, they convinced me. I graciously accepted the pants and put them on. They were a little on the thin side, but it was early fall and still balmy back in Blandon when I arrived, so the risk of me catching my death of cold was low.

My shoes – no two ways around it – were stunning; I'd splurged on them while I was abroad. Nicely heeled, they made a pleasant clopping sound whenever I walked or jogged. Also, they were black and shiny, in an admittedly showy way, with a slight point. As far as finances went, I was not well off, not well off at all, largely due to the fact that I had such an excellent time abroad: eating well, soaking up the interesting cultures, and not worrying about saving the money I was making. Since I was without any means that morning, you might think that I was hungry, my stomach busy eating itself for sustenance, but thankfully this wasn't the case. Before leaving, I had spent some money – the last of it, actually – on a variety of snacks, which, just before boarding the boat, I smartly stuffed into the pockets of my roomy pants. This allowed me to snap off little pieces of my stash during the long journey home, and while pretending to cough I would bring the pieces up to my mouth and discreetly devour them without attracting much notice. Which was a good thing for me to have done, in the end, because everyone else on board was starving.

As my ship inched closer, I also noticed that most of Blandon's oceanfront property was up for sale – the words were legible even from my position offshore – and I was overjoyed, though I tried to put on a grave face. Growing up in Blandon, the beach-dwelling people always rankled me because of their luxurious lifestyles, and though my family was by no means poor, we lived farther inland and didn't go around flaunting our money right there on the beach. However, recent experience had taught me that it was never nice to delight in someone else's property loss, so to change the subject of my thinking I sang a short song to myself, just a little number I picked up when I was abroad.

With arms outstretched, the wavers assisted me onto the dock. I thanked them for supporting me, they thanked me for thanking them, and after shaking hands and embracing for a while I let them get back to their waving. While I tried to be the bigger person with regards to the fisherman – taking his slight in stride and letting it slide off me – I just couldn't help myself, so I wandered over to him. He was sitting with his back to me, his hairy legs dangling right over the dock. I prepared to squat, so as to more easily whisper in his ear, but before I could even begin my descent I was struck by the feeling that underneath all that sea-grime lay someone I knew. I smiled thinly at him, just to see what he would do, and much to my surprise he smiled back, widely, revealing his unusual small, spaced-out teeth, and I then realized with a certain amount of shock that I was staring at my father. It had been years since I'd seen him – he'd long stopped living with my mother and me by the time I decided to go abroad – but he was still, in his way, a hero of mine.

"Hello." I felt compelled to say something and was hoping to wade into the conversation, letting him take it where he wanted. But before he could even reply, something began tugging at his line, and it drew his eyes from me to his rod.

"Well, well, well," he said, "what will I eat today?"

"I hope it's something big," I said, though I couldn't put as much feeling into the words as I wanted.

"Thank you," he said. "Thank you for the fishing wishes." Then, because mere tugging wasn't enough, he stood up and started fighting with the rod. We stared out at the water together. After some struggle, he reeled in his line and closely examined his catch. It was only a wet handkerchief, perhaps one that a waver had let slip while celebrating. He freed the handkerchief from the hook, wrung it out, and tied it around his neck.

"Are you going to return that to its owner?" I said.

"Only if they claim it," he said.

"What if it has sentimental value?"

"Distance swells the heart," he said. "How are you doing?"

"Fine," I said. "Trying to get used to Blandon again."

"Well, where are you coming from?" he said.

"Abroad."

"Oh. And how long have you been away?"

"A few years," I said. "Give or take."

"Give or take?"

"I was out of range for a while," I said, embarrassed. "I kind of lost track of the days."

"If you don't track them, you don't miss them."

"I don't know," I said. "I'd say I already miss them."

"I'll bet you made a whole host of friends, didn't you?"

"Absolutely," I said. "Lifelong friends."

"Make sure to keep in touch with them," he said.

"Oh?"

"Or else they'll feel lonely."

"I will," I said, which was a lie. I had forgotten to collect any phone numbers before leaving.

"So, on the whole, you had a good trip?"

"I did," I said, proudly. "I learned a lot."

"Great."

"It was."

"But Son," he said, looking me right in the eyes. "Something doesn't add up."

"What is it?" I said.

"Well," he said. "If you liked it so much over there – abroad, I mean – why didn't you just stay put?"

"Yeah," I said. "That's a good question. I suppose it never really felt like home – never fully, anyway. Even the moments when I was having the most fun I always felt something calling me back. I missed Blandon. I missed you and Mom."

"Your work dried up, didn't it?" he said.

"How did you know?"

"A father knows," he said. "It's very expensive over there."

"It is," I said. "My money just disappeared."

"I must say I'm quite proud."

"Oh?"

"Not many people ever leave their home state."

I didn't really know what to say at this moment, actually, because my father had never told me he was proud of me before, and I was overcome.

"You must think yourself pretty cultured now," he said.

"I guess so," I said.

"Did you hold on to your values?"

"Values?"

"The ones I instilled in you, when you were young."

"Oh, I think so," I said. I wasn't sure what he was referring to.

"Recite them now," he said. "If you don't mind."

I took several wild guesses: "Truthfulness, steadfastness, transparentness, upstandingness, and willingness."

"You forgot steadfastness."

"Did I?" I said, but went no further – the last thing I wanted to do was fight with my usually absent father. I was eager to leave the conversation anyway, and hoped to end it on a positive note.

"And these values you just recited," he said. "Were you able to force them on others?"

"As often as I could," I said. This was the absolute truth.

"And did you find the people receptive to them?"

"Most of the time, I guess. Have you seen my mother lately?" I suddenly wanted to see her more than anything.

"I have not," he said. "You know how I feel about sharing a bed." Then he launched into a long speech about why this was so.

"I'm going to pay her a visit," I said, and took a high strong step, which, in hindsight, was a thoughtless thing to do, because my shoe clopped on the wooden dock, and my father's attention went to my feet.

"My," he said. "Those are pretty."

"They're functional too."

"And you bought them abroad?"

I nodded. "An impulse buy."

He handed me his fishing rod, then dropped to his knees. After untying the handkerchief, he spat on my shoes and began polishing them.

"You don't have to do that," I said. I must say I did not like the idea of my own father putting his hands all over my feet.

"I'd be honored," he said. "Especially after everything you've done."

"I don't have money to pay you."

"I wouldn't think of asking," he said. "Never, never, never."

"All right," I said.

"Son," he said suddenly. "How in the world did you make ends meet while you were abroad?"

"I worked," I said. "I was employed. Why?"

"I just hope you didn't sign on any dotted lines."

"No?"

"No," he said. "That's how they get you."

"It was mostly just work for hire," I said.

"We're in a slump here," he said. "I don't know how closely you've been following the news."

"I've tried to keep up, but none of my sources have mentioned it."

"Your sources might be biased, then," he said. "Take a look at that beachfront."

I fixed my eyes again on the vacant properties. Of course, seeing all those empty boarded-up homes made me long to see my mother even more.

"Do you know what causes slumps?"

"No."

"One guess."

"Squandered resources," I said. I could not remember where I had learned that.

"Close," he said. "Reckless spending."

"Okay," I said.

I decided to make a run for it and tried putting one foot in front of the other, but my legs didn't properly extend, and I looked down and saw that my father had tied my laces together.

"Is this your standard shine?" I said.

"No," he said, "but I'll give you a good price."

"I told you I don't have any money," I said.

"We'll work something out," he said. "Installments."

I wanted to call out to the wavers for help getting free, but when I craned my neck to look for them, I couldn't find them anywhere.

"What happened to everyone?" I said.

"Do you think I keep tabs on those people?" he said.

Keeping my feet close together, I turned myself slowly around until I saw that all the wavers had lined up single file behind me. Whether they were waiting to get their shoes shined or whether they just liked standing that way, I wasn't sure, and they certainly weren't volunteering information. In fact, they'd given up their waving, smiling, and crying altogether, and were now eyeing us silently. My father, oblivious to the queue, continued his polish job – I could see his wrists and hands poking in between my legs.

"I'd like to go now," I said.

"No, no," he said. "Not yet. You haven't asked me if I have been personally affected by the slump."

57

"Have you?" I said.

"Of course," he said, pointing to an empty cooler nearby.

"Do you usually fill that with fish or with drinks?"

"Well," he said, "it used to be drinks, until that got out of hand and began affecting my fishing."

"Do you miss them?"

"Yes," he said.

"I hope you catch some fish today," I said.

"Me too," he said. "I'd hate to have to hit up your mother."

"She would probably hate that too."

"What are your life plans, Son?"

"I'd like to accomplish a lot," I said.

"Don't you think it's time you found a sweetheart?"

"Maybe," I said. "It's hard to know."

"But you had your fun while abroad?"

"A lot," I said. I considered mentioning some of my flings, then thought better of it.

"So you lost your innocence, I take it?"

"I think so," I said. "Though if it's still around, I bet it's here to stay."

"Beware the substances," he said. "All substances. Drinks *and* drugs."

"I've always been pretty well-adjusted," I said.

"But I gave you the addictive gene."

"I'm not too worried about it," I said.

"Be forewarned."

"I'll try."

"I'm out of advice," he said.

"And I'm going to see the woman who raised me," I said, without much bitterness. "It's been really interesting seeing you." I turned a careful circle again, so that he could see on my face that I meant what I said. He looked up at me and smiled, showing his teeth again.

"All done, Son."

"Can you please tie my laces back to their proper shoes?"

"I can," he said, and then he did just as I asked, pulling the laces free from each other and tying two big beautiful knots, one on each shoe. "Check that rod. Something is nibbling."

Sure enough, there really was something, and I fought with it for a minute, then reeled it in, but after bringing the catch up to my face, I saw that it was just an old shoe, all worn out and water-logged, which only added to the guilt I felt about my own. I looked down again and noticed that my father had no shoes of his own – his gnarly toes told the whole story – so I freed the shoe from the still baited hook and got down on my knees. Taking one of his filthy feet in my hands, I partially shod my father, who seemed grateful, because he put his hands on my shoulders, pulled me up, pulled me close, then brought his mouth up to my ear and whispered: "The only reason I was absent from your upbringing is because your mother and I didn't share the same values that we did before we made you, and I'm telling you this only because I'm very, very hungry and if I'm not able to catch any fish today there's a good chance I will faint and fall forward right off this dock, and except for the small splash my body will make there'll be no evidence that I was ever here at all except of course my rod and my cooler and that part of me that you carry within yourself, and the last thing I would want is for you to live your life hating that part of yourself because I didn't take the time to tell you that I had nothing against you while we were both still alive."

Though he found it necessary to speak with his tongue in my ear, he was still, in his way, a hero of mine, so I stuck out my hand, and he stuck out his hand, and we shook them together, as friends do, and when he released me from his grasp I reached in my pocket and broke him off a piece of what I had. I told him to kneel down and open wide, which he did, his new shoe tucked beneath him, and then I jammed the cracker into his mouth. His eyes lit up, and he seemed to savor it, and it felt so good to see him happy that I ended up giving him a whole cracker, which I really shouldn't have done because the wavers were still watching us closely. I could have never guessed that they were hungry too, but they surrounded my father and me, and closed in on us quickly, smiling wider and crying louder and waving faster than they had when I arrived, and if I hadn't had somewhere else to be, I would have gladly stayed and defended that cracker with my father, but my mother was calling me, and it was time for me to be home. I forced my way through the wavers and jogged briskly down the pier.

THE MOUTH

— You like it, huh?

— What?

— The river.

— Love it.

— It's pretty nasty in the daytime.

— It ain't daytime now.

— Fog's nice too, huh?

— Like a pall.

— I tell you about my dream?

— The one about the rat?

— A new one. You finished with that bottle?

— Not yet.

— So, I'm swimming in the river.

— This one here?

— That's right. I'm naked and by myself.

— Uh-huh.

— And everything's good, I'm swimming to my heart's content, but then my arms and legs get heavy.

— Can't swim with heavy limbs. You yelling?

— Screaming like a bitch.

— But you don't die?

— No, something comes to my aid.

— Lucky duck. What?

— I'll give you a hint: it floats when it bloats.

— That's a body.

— A cadaver, yeah.

— Dick or slit?

— Can't tell, it's facedown.

— But naked?

— Naked, yeah.

— It assists you?

— I see it come by, so I grab it.

— With those heavy hands?

— Well, they get lighter.

— Nice, all right. Is it buoyant?

— Yeah. I swing my legs over, sit up on it.

— On that dead ass?

— Yeah, cheek to cheek.

— You ride it, huh?

— I'm bobbin' up and down.

— How's it feel?

— Squishy.

— And the smell?

— Pure putrefaction.

— But the ride's good?

— Unlike anything.

— You take it back to shore?

— Nope, downstream.

— A little ways?

— A long ways.

— Past the refineries?

— All the way to the mouth, baby.

— Then what?

— I pass out on the sand.

— And the body?

— It just sorta sinks.

— Sounds like a good dream.

— It was.

— You wake up wet?

— You know it. What you think it means?

— Means drown a little, gain a lot. Means get the dead beneath you. Means out of bad, good.

— Yeah. I tell you my sister visited last week?

— Little Miss Uptight? What did she want?

— Just checking up on baby bro.

— Think she suspects anything?

— No. I was double careful.

— How was it?

— Good. Did some drinking.

— Family's family.

— That's right.

— You glad you moved back here?

— Oh, definitely.

— It's as crazy as you remember it?

— Crazier.

— Gonna be crazy for a while too.

— I know. Not many crazy places left.

— Getting to be a real clean country.

— So are we doing this?

— Yeah, let's get to it.

— Big day tomorrow, huh? Parade rolls at nine.

— You know I'll be ready.

— Don't forget your mask, madman.

— Never do.

— Pass me that bottle, would you?

— You bet.

— And do it gentle this time, all right?

— All right.

FIRST GHOST STORY

No one has ever asked me to tell a ghost story before, but that's not so surprising: do I seem like the type of person who would carry a flesh-creeping tale around in his head? You can always spot these sorts – their anxious, inward aspects give them away – and they're very unnerving to be around. Maybe I have a story, maybe not. Are ghost stories really still told and enjoyed? Doubtful, I think. But someone wants a ghost story tonight, and I say, why not.

A few years ago, I found myself in a very dark place. I worked long irregular hours for a company I hated; my romantic relationships were all coming to abrupt and ugly ends; and one night, when I thought my anxiety couldn't rise any higher, my apartment caught fire, and though I tried to wake each of my sleeping roommates before seeing myself to safety, every one of them burned, and had a faulty outlet not been fingered as the culprit, I would have been on the streets. I filed a lawsuit against my landlord and won easily, receiving a very generous check. I suddenly had the freedom to do as I pleased.

But what did I want to do? I knew I needed to get away: from my boring city, from my hideous job, from my burnt apartment and my deceased roommates – whose screams were finding their way into my dreams – but I didn't know where I wanted to go. How stupidly complicating money can be sometimes! I wanted to stay in the United States, but I also wanted some place fresh and exotic. After a bit of research, I settled on New Orleans. Many were put off by my choice, understandably – the city's reputation as a den of disease, decay, and alcoholic dependency did not help them in seeing the positives. In the end, I had no good answer for them.

I just wanted to go to New Orleans. I moved down, found an apartment with lots of atmosphere, and filled it with fantastic things. I made friends instantly and filled my nights with drinking, dancing, and doing drugs. I took all kinds of lovers too, refusing to bow to traditional notions. In short: I lived like the full-blooded man I was born to be.

And then one morning it was all over. Mardi Gras was in full swing, the whole city deep in a weeklong debauch, but I was on the floor of my apartment – dying. My teeth were chattering and I could feel the death throes coursing through me. So it had come to this. A tragic but life-affirming accident, a generous settlement, a year of high but uncareful living, and now the end. I heard the anguished voices of my old roommates in my head, and I knew I wouldn't be long in joining them.

But then I started gurgling with laughter, because I remembered something important. You see, in reality, I had died in the apartment fire that night, alongside my roommates; I did not get out in time. Clearly I had not wanted to accept this, so I invented the story about the lawsuit and the settlement, tricking my dead brain into believing that I needed to apply the laws of the living to my new situation – that I needed food, that I needed clothes, that I needed love and perhaps a roof over my head. You laugh, but put yourself in my shoes for a moment. It was so awful to burn alive. The flames raced toward me, the smoke tore at my lungs, I smelled my own charred flesh – you would have tried to forget it too. But please understand: I really did make it down to New Orleans, really did have a wild and matchless time there; it just so happened to have occurred after I was dead.

JUMBLES

I was sitting alone in my apartment, on the green couch, the one that had caused me so much trouble as of late, and I was typing out a goodbye email to Dee on my laptop. The overhead lights were all turned off; in fact, the only light in the room was coming from my screen. I'd just packed up everything I owned and loaded it in my car, and was doing this one last thing as a courtesy to Dee before leaving. It was cold in the room – my hands were trembling and my fingers weren't always striking the right keys. But I was determined to get it all out, before I changed my mind.

I basically wanted to apologize to him for the way I had acted at the bar earlier, and to tell him that no matter what happened, I would always think of him as a good roommate. I also wanted to tell him how happy I was that he had made some good friends, and how good it made me feel to see him having fun with them earlier that evening. Obviously things hadn't been going as well for me – the last few weeks I had been feeling more unwell every day – but now I was leaving, and no amount of begging could make me stay.

But just before I could press send, I heard keys jingling outside the door. I scrambled to appear natural: I snapped my laptop closed, set it down on the coffee table, and sat back on the couch. Then I realized just how odd it would appear if he found me sitting in complete darkness, so I reached over and brought the laptop back to my lap, opened it, and pulled up a news article. I put my hand to my chin and pretended to be immersed in my reading. The door swung open, and I saw Dee in silhouette, backlit by a streetlamp. I could tell by the way he swayed that he had been doing some drinking. Of course, I'd been drinking too, but not so much that it was going to impair the driving I would soon be doing.

"Hey," he said, in a froggy voice. He shut the door behind him and locked it very slowly, bending down to watch the bolt slide home.

"Oh, hey Dee," I said, trying to smile naturally.

"Late-night reading?"

"Yeah, just relaxing before bed."

"That's nice," he said. "No pajamas tonight?"

"No," I said, "probably just sleep in my clothes."

"Me too. It's cold in here."

"Yeah."

"Mind if I turn on the heat?"

"Go ahead," I said.

He went over to the heater, sparked it a few times, then gave it a little gas. Soon there were little blue flames dancing in the grate and a bit more light in the room. He warmed his backside for a few moments, taking deep breaths with his eyes closed. I watched him from over my laptop, feeling relieved he hadn't seen how crammed my car was.

"That's better," he said. "Oh yeah, this feels so, so good."

"I'll bet," I said. Then, to distract him, I asked him how the rest of the night was.

"Good," he said. "After trivia ended, we threw darts for a while."

"That's nice. Sorry I left so suddenly."

"It's all right," he said, breaking into one of his coughing fits. When he recovered, he said, "They're not really your kind of people, I know."

"They're just different," I said.

"Different, yeah," he said, smiling slightly. "We still have that bottle of Jumbles around?"

"No, sorry. I drank it all earlier."

"That's all right. Mind if I sit for a minute? Just for a second before I go to sleep?"

"No, I don't mind." Of course, I did mind, what with all my possessions and valuables on display outside to anyone passing by. But I had a feeling our talk would be brief. I set the laptop on the coffee table and closed it, which darkened the room considerably. Dee shuffled over to the available side of the couch, then fell back onto the green cushions.

"How's she doing?" Dee said, nodding toward my laptop.

"Not so great," I said. "Just hoping to get a few more months out of her. How's yours?"

"Still got that crack," he said. "Which isn't getting any smaller."

"Yeah, that's not what cracks do, I guess."

"Oh well," he said. "When it goes, it goes."

"That's the truth," I said.

"You sure you're doing all right, Milky?" That was his nickname for me, which I tolerated.

"Yeah, I'm all right," I lied.

Dee did one of his signature moves then and swooped his hair back, and in doing so revealed a large bump on his left temple. There was some dried blood caked all around it, but it was the size that was the most alarming.

"What happened to your head, Dee?"

"I fell, I guess."

"Where?"

"On the tracks," he said. "Near the glass piles."

"Yikes," I said.

"It's just a bump. You can touch it if you want."

"Nah," I said. "You didn't black out, did you?"

"I remember tripping and going down, and then I remember sitting up, holding my head."

"Do you think we should go to the hospital?" I said, hoping he'd turn me down.

"I'll be fine."

"Well, that's good. I guess we all fall sometimes."

"Yeah," he said. "And anyway, it's you I'm more worried about."

"Me?" I said. "I'm doing A-OK, Dee."

"You've been acting strange lately."

"That's weird," I said. "I think I've been acting normal."

"No, I wouldn't say so."

"Well, what have I been doing that's strange?"

"You don't look me in the eye anymore. Also, your fingers won't stop twitching and your voice keeps cracking. And you're drinking a lot, more than you usually do."

"Well, so are you," I said.

"It's different," he said, "I drink for pleasure, and to relax. You're drinking out of discomfort."

"Well, I don't know about that, Dee," I said. "I think I'm doing just fine."

"Maybe," he said. "Have you heard from Kaye lately?"

"No, thank God," I said. Kaye was the girl I had been dating in the last town Dee and I had lived in, who had followed me down here in the hopes of being with me, even though I had told her to stay put. She rented an apartment nearby, and while I did my best to avoid her, there were some nights when I couldn't help but run into her at the bar. We would have a few drinks and catch up, and then we would come back to the apartment and fool around on the green couch, the same one that Dee and I were now sitting on.

"Do you love her?" Dee said.

"Yeah, I do," I said. "Sometimes I wish she hadn't followed me down here, but that's what happened. I guess we're just sort of figuring it out. But I'm glad we aren't boyfriend and girlfriend anymore."

"Yeah," Dee said, placing a hand on my shoulder. "With Clary it's the same – we're just kinda figuring it out." Clary was the girl that Dee had been dating and who he was trying to detach from, even though there were a few nights when I'd walked in on them fooling around on the green couch as well.

"I guess we're both a little confused right now," I said.

"Of course we are," he said, beginning to massage my shoulder. "And I'm sure last Tuesday didn't help things."

"No, it sure didn't, Dee!" I said, jumping up from the couch. "Last Tuesday didn't help things at all!"

"Come on, Milky, sit back down. Don't lose your head."

"I'm fine," I said, regaining composure and sitting back down.

We sat in silence for a few moments, and I occasionally stole glances at Dee, whose head had fallen back onto the couch. He was staring at the ceiling, and the shadowy light from the heater was dancing all over the bump.

"Are you sure you're all right, Dee?"

With some effort, he rolled his head back upright, then turned to look at me.

"Of course. It's just the end of the night. You sure we don't have that bottle of Jumbles around anywhere?"

"Positive," I said.

"Guess we'll just have to do without."

"Maybe that's not so bad."

"But tell me, Milky," he said, his hand suddenly on my thigh. "How do you feel about what happened last Tuesday?"

"You mean what happened after the bar?" I said, hoping that wasn't in fact the thing he wanted to talk about.

"Exactly," he said.

The incident Dee was referring to was this: last Tuesday, he and I had been out at the bar, and when it closed, we came back to our apartment and made a little food. After finishing it, both of us sat down at either end of the couch, reading the news on our laptops and digesting. All of a sudden we looked up from our laptops and locked eyes, set our laptops down on the coffee table, and started fooling around. After a little while, we stopped, retreated back to our opposite sides of the couch, brought our laptops back to our laps, and began reading the news as if nothing had happened.

"I don't know," I said. "I guess I feel like it was a pretty weird thing that happened."

"You think so?"

"I do. It was just a weird thing for us to do all of a sudden."

"Which part?" he said. "When we were kissing, or when we were licking each other's butts?"

"Well, all of it, I guess," I said. "You didn't think it was a weird thing to be doing?"

"The only part that was weird for me," said Dee, "was how floppy we both were the whole time. That was frustrating."

"Yeah," I said. "Do you think that maybe our hearts weren't in it?"

"I think we'd just had too much gin," Dee said. "Next time, I bet we'll be nice and hard."

"I guess," I said. "But I don't want to do that again, Dee."

"No?" he said, real disappointment crossing his face.

"I just can't see it," I said. "Besides, I'm still sorting out my feelings for Kaye."

"I see."

"And anyway," I said, "I don't think roommates should fool around together. Remember Geril and Leddy?"

"Of course."

"Well, they were roommates and they fooled around, and that was horrific, how that ended."

"That's not the same. Geril's time overseas was the cause of that."

"I don't know," I said. "I think it was the fact that they were roommates."

"Okay, Milky, have it your way."

"Besides," I said. "Aren't you still sorting out your feelings for Clary?"

"Of course," he said. "But that has to do with my heart."

"I guess I don't know what you mean."

"In my heart," Dee continued, "I'm still really confused. But in my penis, I feel free and easy."

"Are they really such separate things?"

"They are," Dee said.

"I don't know," I said. "Seems to me like they've always worked together, gone hand in hand."

"Maybe we can make them work together," Dee said, winking at me.

"What do you mean?"

"You and me, Milky. Penis and heart."

"Nah, Dee. But thanks for asking."

"Come on, let's fool around for a minute."

"No thanks, Dee."

"Please?"

"No, Dee."

"Sometime soon, then?"

I took a good look at him, and found my eyes settling once again on his bloody bump.

"No," I said. "That was a one-time thing, and I'm sorry if it left you wanting more."

"You're pretty good at it," he said.

"Well, thanks," I said.

"I think you could make a few fast friends if you kept working at it."

"Good night, Dee."

He pulled me close and gave me a very wet kiss on the cheek. Then he got up, stretched and scratched himself, and stumbled toward the pocket doors. "Good night, you poor son of a bitch," he said.

When he was gone, I leaned back against the sofa and resumed typing my email.

I LEAD A PLEASANT LIFE

You may say I've lost my mind, living here, but I ask you friend, who needs a mind? God loves a simple soul, and here I am, nice and simple and loving life. A cool breeze blowing through my head, a nice airy feeling deep inside. This city appeals to me, has always appealed to people like me, people with a disposition gentle as mine. And I've gotten nice and fat just being me – now haven't I?

Do I *have* an apartment? Do I *need* an apartment? It's always sunny down on the street. Most days I just lie on the sidewalk, reclining on my side. The sun burns my skin pink, but I don't mind – I do what I want to do. Raise a finger, roll my eyes, whatever comes to mind.

The barbershop boys, they offer me work sometimes. They say, "Hey Bobby Boy, we got a job that needs doing, an crrand that needs running."

And I say, from where I lay, "Well now, speak slowly and come a little closer."

And they say, "We'll pay, we'll pay."

And I say, "So what is it that must be done?"

"Some nasty old man is flapping his lips across town," they say, "and we need you to sew his mouth shut."

Or, "That crusty lady over there needs bus fare, bring her some."

Or, "Mop up that spot right quick, but shut your eyes tight the whole time."

Sure, I listen politely, but then I just wave them away.

And yet there are some that would seek to destroy my peace. Just yesterday, a skinny little man in a delicate hat spotted me on the sidewalk. He'd just left Mulley Mutual, and it was plain to see his pockets were loaded. I was just minding my own business, eating an ice cream cone – vanilla, of course – and it was melting and dripping all down my hand.

"Did you hear the news?" he said.

"Is it good?" I said.

"A waiter got shot up today on Lampeen Street," he said, "and later on, in Terko, an evil child garroted his own father. How can you lie there and eat cream while all this is going on?"

Well, what do you think I told him? I'm a sensitive soul, at my center. What could I, what could anyone, say to that? I was guilty, guilty as charged. There I was, lying back, taking pleasure in dairy, while nearby, dark things were going on. While I was taking my bites, a young father was losing his life. I said nothing; I crumpled. I dropped my cone on the ground, put my head in my hands, and cried.

But out of bad came good, and soon I felt a smooth hand on my shoulder. It belonged to the skinny man, and do you know what he was holding in his other hand? A brand-new ice cream cone, and he handed it to me. Suffice to say, it wasn't long before the tears started flowing again, dropping all salty on my vanilla. I smiled a grateful smile. Then, right before I took a lick, I made sure to think about poor old mankind.

But it has been a pleasant life, didn't I say it has? Though far, far from over – I'm in terrific health. I had such a fine upbringing too, and God knows, not every person can say that. My mother was such a caring, careful woman, and my father? He never laid a hairy hand on me. My sister – my sweet, sexy sister – it's true she idolized me, always wished she could be more like me, but she loved money too much, and in the end it cost her her life. But it makes me smile to know she's resting in peace now, alongside Mommy and Daddy.

It's always a good day when the taco truck comes rolling by, and if I have a little loose change, I flag the woman down. My goodness, what a scrumptious mamacita she is – such a pleasure to watch her fire up the grill and fix four fresh tacos just for me – extra cheese, please.

"You dropped a drop of cream back there, miss," I say, just to get her smiling. "But wait, I found it here, sliding down your back-side. Oh, and bring me more of that green sauce I like so much, and if I smear it where you fear it, don't judge me too much. Spicy radish pickle lady, I want to tickle your happy labey – let me eat my taco inside your taco. I just had four, but now I'll have four more. I'll eat tacos till I burst and spew forth, and then you, you angel, you'll stitch me up and fix some more."

Oh my God, she makes me say the most foolish, lovelorn things – and she must feel good about the power she wields. Women don't get enough credit for the way they wield their power, I believe that's true, and I'd like to change that if I could.

Some days are just too warm for clothes – they stick to me and give me a touch of anxiety, and I get a red rash, from my ankles to my hips. And there isn't but one way to treat a recurring rash: you've got to air yourself out – and what's more, you've got to do it without any shame or doubt. Let mother nature do the work she was made to do. Let her breeze cool your irritated skin, let her yellow sun just bake the pain away. Some mornings you might see my pants and tighty-whities folded neatly beside me, and my sizable genitals on display, and I wouldn't mind if you waved.

But a man must know his limits, all the same. And if on a rashy day I see a yellow bus coming, bearing those bright faces off to a day of punishing instruction, I flip over and show them my behind. Sure, the children laugh – don't think I can't hear those pealing squeals, echoing all up and down the block – but let them, I say, let them laugh the whole day away for all I care, I'll be their itchy downtown clown, it's a small price to pay.

Never in my life have I been the kind to profile, but just recently it happened to me. Can you believe it? Bobby Boy got himself profiled the other day, and the results may surprise you.

I was just doing my thing, the thing I always do – reclining and smiling on the smoky hot sidewalk in the middle of the day – when two patrolmen pulled their cruiser over to the curb. They popped open the doors and made a beeline for me.

"You don't mind if we ask you a few questions?" they said, the classic come-on.

"About what?" I said. "I haven't done anything wrong."

"We're looking for a pink man," they said, "about your size and girth. Been terrorizing this neighborhood these last few weeks."

"Gentlemen," I said, having a little fun, "just because I fit *a* description, doesn't mean I fit *the* description, and just because my crust is rosy, doesn't mean I'm guilty – of a crime."

"We never thought of it that way," they said. Then they commenced beating me.

I won't lie: sometimes I make up people in my mind, people that aren't really there, that I'm conjuring with my imagination. You might call them my imaginary friends, but I say, are my friends so imaginary if what they wreak is real? What if they make me feel the same things that real people do? How imaginary is that? There's a baby, for example, that dangles from the streetlight, by means of a ratty blanket, and he gurgles all sorts of nonsense and funny things.

His name is Baby Light.

And sometimes there's this old fellow that pops out from behind the garbage cans. He doesn't say much, but he raises his eyebrows a bunch and he's got ketchup stains all over his suit. I call him Red Man, and if you want to know, I use him as comic relief. And I won't even tell you about Gally Holiday and her horse, which she rides backward, butt-naked. Most times I see them at night, or in the early morning. Then again, it's not uncommon for me to see them after waking from my afternoon nap.

But Spider, he's the man with the plan. Bald and bold and white as a dove, he's always running a dream and a funny little scheme. He owns the furniture shop across the street, which, in my opinion, is just a front. How do I know this? Well, there's never not some dirty truck backing up to his front door, never not some drugged-up, goofy-smiling duck stumbling out into the bright sunshine.

Spider comes to see me around lunchtime, plops right down next to me with a fat sandwich and a sigh.

"How's the day looking, Bobby Boy?" he'll say. "Gonna be in the hundreds, they're saying."

"Oh, fine," I say. "I hope so."

"You sure love that direct sun, don't you?" he says. "Better be careful or it'll fry your mind."

"I've been cooking here twenty years," I say. "And if today is the day, so be it, I don't mind. I live a pleasant life, and you can see it on my face."

"That's a good attitude," he says. "It'll take you far in this old world."

"It already has," I say. "It already has."

And what happens when it rains, you ask, when God sends a little blessed water down? It isn't any terrible thing. A little rain's always welcome – it rinses the skin *and* the soul. I open my mouth and catch the fat drops on my tongue, and remember back to days when I was young. When I was just a timid little squit, living in the shitty Midwest. Before I hopped aboard that flaming barge, bound for the sunny South.

But if that sprinkle should become torrential, I roll myself under the awning, taking care not to touch the broken bottles. The barbershop boys, they know the drill. They know that when it pours, Bobby Boy is going to keep extra close.

Now when the city does its cleaning of the streets – when they send those spinning brooms down the block – that's the time I've got to be on guard. Once I slept through such a cleaning and woke up with one of my nipples hanging off. Wasn't Bobby Boy a sight that night, a full-grown man screaming like a bitch on the sidewalk, with one of his pink nippies shorn?

Would you like to hear a little tale? Why not, I'll just make something up. This is a story about a man named Sal. Sal, short for Salami Smith, at least that's what his friends called him. Sal, you see, had himself a pink pal, and his name was BB. BB and Sal, they were practically brothers, sidewalk sleepers and midnight bleepers, on a block not unlike this one, but this was a long time ago. There wasn't no Mulley Mutual then, no sandwich shop neither. Only block after block of burned-out houses with no trees to speak of.

BB and Sal, they used to lie in the street together, and they shared everything: dairy, ladies, you name it – there wasn't anything that passed through BB that didn't pass through Sal. But Sal, he had issues; he couldn't live free like BB. He fell under the spell of something malignant, started acting like anything but himself. Then he started using hard drugs and hanging out in those ugly houses. Poor Sal, every day he was becoming more and more emaciated, every day his pink skin turned more and more blue. Soon he quit the street altogether. He disappeared in one of those houses for good, until the day they carried him out.

Oh, Sal, where are you right now? Are you in heaven, smiling down? Or are you in hell, sweating all your evil out? The end. I hope you liked my little tale. I sure enjoyed telling it to you.

I have observed the mating habits of rats, my friends, and I am here to say that they are tender with each other. Roaches, too, they are very attentive lovers. And when the pigeons fly down from Mulley Mutual for some screwing, first they do a little necking. Street dogs are different, though, it seems to me, and much less lovely to watch. The male is often cold and aggressive, mounting a female before she even has time to know what's going on.

But as for me? My love comes to see me at sunset, when all the bright neon is fizzling on. She makes her money in a restaurant and always brings a fresh tablecloth with her, and under the cloth we get it on. She's got sweet cheeks and a big round butt, and a throat that's lined with gold. What a creature, what a teacher, we play for hours together.

Can you imagine, just the other day, some stranger thought he recognized me? In my opinion, it's the age we live in. Everyone knows everyone else, and there just isn't any distance between you and me.

He said, "I know you. You're Jack Sprack, disgraced CEO of Mulley Mutual."

And I said, "You most definitely have the wrong man. My name is Bobby Boy, and I live on the street."

And believe you me he left me alone.

A motorcyclist died today, but really, what can you say? He had a need for speed; he had a drive for the wild side. He blew through a red light, and got T-boned by a family man in a minivan out for a pleasant Sunday drive. His helmet popped off and went skidding by, and pieces of his brain flecked me where I lay. It wasn't so shocking: you live your life, you dance your dance, then, one day, you pass on. Maybe you pass on quick, maybe nice and slow, but it was decided, long before you opened your eyes, that one day you must pass on. And for me that's a comfort, the fact that we all share that.

When I die, and as I've said, this will not be for a long, long time, just leave me be. This is Bobby Boy's last wish. Leave my body on the sidewalk for all to see. When I'm freshly dead, there will be no fuss or muss, I'll look just like I did in life, but with my eyes kindly closed. This is the time to come see me, to pay your last respects. You may have to stand in line awhile – you might have to wait behind the mamacita and the barbershop boys and Spider and all the rest – but soon enough you'll get your turn. Kiss me or give my dick a squeeze, lick my neck or smack my butt, however you like to say goodbye. Because before long, I'll start to smell, and the rodents will come running. They'll eat my eyes, they'll gnaw my toes, they'll nibble my lips – they'll have a nice little meal, won't they? Then I'll bloat a little and release my juices. Soon I'll lose my mass, and a pink puddle will start to form. Do steer clear during these times. But on the day – surely so very far away – when all my flesh is gone, and it's only my pretty white bones reclining on the sidewalk, go ahead and sweep old Bobby Boy into the street. Remember him as someone who lived simply, one hundred percent dedicated to the pleasant life.

Every single day I watch those happy travelers line up across the street. All those searching souls, sitting on their black bags, waiting patiently for the dollar bus to arrive. Just a dollar, they say, and you can go anywhere you care to stay. North, east, west, you can leave no stone in this fair country unturned, no mile unmarked, all for a dollar. It makes a man like me curious, and curiously jealous, sometimes. I've thought about taking it a couple times, and maybe I will go someday, leave this greasy street behind. Hoist myself up into the bus, pop my dollar into the machine, and say to that driver, "To think is to stink, my good man, so take me far from my dollar mind."

HEARD FROM WEST

I.

It was while on my run that evening that I started to get worried – it had been about forty-eight hours since I'd last heard from West. He'd recently moved from my apartment, where he'd been crashing since he moved to town, to another nearby – a friend of my co-worker had rented it to him. I hadn't been inside the new place yet, but I knew where it was because I'd biked him home after a movie three days before.

On that ride we'd talked not only about the movie, but about a book West had just finished, written by an author we both liked, who wrote obsessively about dark subjects – madness and suicide mostly. I hadn't read that one, but I'd read others, and as we biked beside each other West described the ways in which he identified with the protagonist, and when we got to the gate – his was a small stand-alone unit behind the main house – I wished him good night, and that was the last time we'd spoken. I'd called him on my way to the coffee shop earlier but he hadn't picked up.

When I got back from the run I greeted my roommate, who was in the kitchen cooking, then went to my room to check my phone. There was nothing from West, so before getting in the shower I asked my roommate if he'd heard from him in the last few days. He said he hadn't, which wasn't surprising – I was closer to West than he was – so I tried to take that with a grain of salt. But in the shower I definitely grew more worried – the thing that flashed across my mind was the expression West had worn one afternoon lying on my air mattress, when he didn't think anyone was looking at him . . .

I threw on some clothes and told my roommate I was going to the store for some essentials, then headed out. I got in my car and headed down North Rampart, and when I got to Congress I turned right and parked. I called West's phone again, but it rang and rang and then reverted to his greeting: "It's West. Leave your mess. Goodbye." I decided to knock at the main house, whose door was up a short flight of stairs.

"Who is it?"

"Hey," I said, "It's Matthew, West's friend. I gave him the reference. We were supposed to go to a movie tonight, but he's not answering his phone. Would you mind letting me in the gate?"

"Okay," she said. "Just give me a second."

The landlord was a beautiful woman in her early forties, and when she opened the door, the smell of cooking wafted out.

"I'm sorry about this, by the way."

"It's all right. Let me get my keys."

When she returned she said, "I haven't seen him much since he moved in, but he did pay rent right away."

"That's good," I said.

"He seems like a nice guy."

"Yeah, he's a good guy," I said. Then I said, "They don't make many like West," which sounded strange and I regretted it.

She unlocked the gate. "Great," I said, "thanks again."

"No problem," she said. "Be careful back there. My kids tend to leave their toys out."

"No worries," I said, starting down the path. A little light from inside her house fell onto the scabby grass, which helped me avoid the toy cars and, a little farther on, a sprung jack-in-the-box.

When the studio came into full view, my worry definitely increased. West's inside lights were all on, and the rusty bicycle I had lent him was chained to the fence. He didn't own a car – he had used my Honda to move his stuff – so the bike being there was not the best of signs. I knocked at the door, then went over to the window and peered in, past the knotted curtain. His laptop lay open on a small desk, and there was tea steeping on the countertop in a translucent pot. I could see almost every inch of the place, except inside the bathroom – its door was tightly closed. A light was on in there as well – I could see it shining through the gaps at the top and bottom – and what worried me more was that his favorite pair of house shoes were just outside the door, their toes pointed right at it.

When I knocked at the landlord's door again, she opened it quickly this time, and I said, with a bit more of a tremor than I'd hoped: "I'm sorry, he's not answering his door, which is strange because he seems to be home. Would you mind unlocking it? I actually haven't heard from him in a little while and I've started to get worried."

"How long?"

"Not too long," I said. "Maybe a day or so."

"I thought you said you were going to a movie."

"Well, that wasn't really true. I just didn't want to worry you over nothing."

"I see," she said.

"Anyway, it's probably nothing. His phone probably died."

"Well," she said, "I don't know. You said it's been about a day?"

"Maybe more like two," I said. "But it's probably nothing."

"I hope so. You're not some sort of criminal, are you?"

"No, no, don't worry."

"All right."

We went down the path together. She apologized about the toys, moving some out of the way with her feet. "How well do you know him?" she said.

"Really well. We've been friends since grad school."

"I'm uncomfortable with this."

"Yeah, it's a little weird."

"There are lots of things I don't like about being a landlord."

"I understand. But believe me, West is the kind of guy who wouldn't mind if you let a good friend into his room."

"The lights are on," she said.

"They are," I said, knocking loudly. We waited, heard nothing, then she abruptly put her key in and unlocked it.

"Thanks a lot," I said. "I'll take it from here."

"You sure?" she said, a little perplexed.

"Yeah, I'm sure," I said. "Thanks again."

"Okay," she said. "I'll just be putting the kids down. Let me know if you need anything."

"Sure," I said, "I appreciate it."

I waited until I couldn't hear her anymore, then I opened the door. Its hinge was broken, and it groaned horribly. I closed it behind me, but not all the way.

West was right: it was a very small place, and also, I could now see, quite shabby, with a good layer of grime on the baseboards. But he had moved in: he'd stacked his books at the foot of the bed, hung his clothes on the rack, and even put some of his orange rind sculptures on the wall. "Hey, West," I said in the silence, my hair standing on end. "West, are you in here?" I walked to the small desk where his laptop sat, then over to the bathroom. That door was white, inset with four rectangular panels. "Hey, West!" I said. "West, are you in there?" As I started to turn the handle, I heard a voice say from inside – low and theatrical and definitely West's – "Open this door and be damned! Damned!" I yanked my hand away and leapt back, tripping over his house shoes.

II.

"Jesus, West!" I said. "You scared the shit out of me! Are you all right?"

"All right?" he said. "Yes, of course I'm all right. Why wouldn't I be all right?"

"I don't know. I mean, you haven't been answering your phone. Or your door."

"Am I not entitled to a little privacy now and then?"

"Of course you are. I was just worried, that's all."

"Takes a worried man to sing a worried song," he said, and I could almost see the ironic look on his face. "But tell me, why would you be worried about your old friend West?"

"Very funny," I said. "Listen, are you sure you're all right and don't need any help?"

"I *am* all right and I don't need any help," he said. "But I would appreciate it if you answered my question."

"Why don't you come out of there? I'd feel a lot better if I could see you."

"The answer first, please."

"All right, fine," I said. "I *was* worried, and I still *am* worried, because I know you haven't been in the best of places lately."

"Your evidence is strong. What could one possibly say in response?"

"You don't need to say anything, so long as you're all right."

"Oh, I'm all right," he said.

"So you'll come out now?"

"Not now. But maybe in a little while."

"I can live with that. What are you doing in there, anyway?"

"Just hanging out," he said. "I hope you'll forgive me for not inviting you in."

"It's okay. Do you mind if I have some of that tea?"

"I wouldn't drink that if I were you."

"No?"

"It's not so fresh," he said.

"Okay, well maybe I'll clean the pot and make some more."

"If you want to," he said. "I'm fine, myself."

"Maybe I won't make tea," I said, feeling oppressed by the thought of cleaning. "It's really strange talking to you like this, West."

"It is. But you'll admit that when we roomed together, it wasn't uncommon for us to speak through doors."

"Maybe not," I said. "But still, this feels different."

"You could try to relax a little."

"Relax?"

"You could sit down," he said. "You could take off your coat."

"No, I don't think so. It's pretty chilly in here."

"Yes, I know."

"Do you have a heater?"

"Yes, yes," he said, his voice farther away.

"Well, where is it?"

"It's in here. With me."

"Okay. How long have you been in there, anyway?"

"Too long. I hope you won't judge me harshly."

"I wouldn't do that."

"Even if I'd done something gross?"

"No, I wouldn't judge. What have you done?"

"I ate a meal in here. Two, actually."

"I guess that is a little gross," I said. "But people bring their phones into the bathroom these days, so what do I know?"

"I have that in here too."

"So you saw my calls?"

"I told you I needed my privacy."

"Well, you sure picked a good spot," I said.

"Small and snug," West said. "Safe and secure."

"Right."

"What about music?" West said. "Music might help."

"Sure, I could put on some music." I went over to the desk and pressed a key on the laptop. Its screen snapped back to life. A movie resumed playing – sound and all – and I frantically clicked off the window, but not before a few moans escaped.

"Are you snooping out there? That would make me very sad indeed."

"No. A movie came up on the computer."

"I see," he said. "What sort?"

"To be honest, I think it was some sort of porn."

"Porn?" said West. "Porn?"

"Yeah, I'm afraid so."

"Well, it *is* late in the evening, isn't it?"

"It's getting there," I said, laughing and shaking my head.

"Forgive me for asking, but what kind would you say it was?"

"It seemed pretty hardcore to me."

"And were you able to determine a theme?"

"A theme?"

"Yes," he said. "Even in porn there are themes."

"I only saw for a second. But if I had to guess, I'd say it had to do with humiliation."

"The strangest things cheer us, don't they?"

"Yeah," I said sadly.

"I hope you don't feel ashamed."

"No. It's okay."

"Thank you," said West. "You were going to choose some music, weren't you?"

"Oh yeah, that's right. What do you feel like hearing?"

"Something creepy," said West.

"Creepy? Why?"

"I'd be lying if I said I wasn't feeling a little creepy tonight."

"I thought you said you were fine."

"I *am* fine," he said. "But all the same, I do feel a little creepy. Also, I've been hearing noises outside."

"Noises? What kind?"

"Laughter, mostly. The landlord's kids, I suppose. I don't know why they disturbed me the way they did."

"I wouldn't worry about them."

"If you say so."

"Are you sure you want to listen to creepy music?"

"I'm sure," he said. "But it should be something you like as well."

"That shouldn't be hard," I said – our music libraries were nearly identical.

I sat down at the desk and scrolled through a good number of songs before settling on something. It was a droning song, a long one that actually decayed as it played, though I had always found it more meditative than creepy.

"How's that?" I said.

"It will do."

"Good. Do you want to come out now?"

"First, I need your opinion on something."

"All right, what?"

"Now that you've finally seen it," he said, "what do you think of my new house?"

I took another look around, which basically confirmed everything I had already decided earlier. I didn't want to be critical, so I said, "I think it's pretty great, West. It's small, but homey. And it seems like you've really moved in, with your books around the bed and your orange rind sculptures on the walls."

"I don't like it at all."

"No? It seems like you've got everything you need here."

"It's so dirty and narrow," he said, his voice rasping. "You know what it reminds me of, don't you?"

Just then I heard a knock at the front door.

94

III.

"Should I answer it?" I whispered.

"I would inquire first. Best not to take chances."

"Right," I said, moving to the door. "Who is it?"

"Hey, it's me." I recognized the landlord's voice.

"Oh, just a minute." I opened the door, and it made another horrible sound.

"Hi," she said.

"Hi," I said. "How's it going?"

"Fine. Is everything okay?"

"Everything's okay. He's in the bathroom, and we've been talking."

"Okay, good. That's a relief."

"Yeah, that's where he's at," I said, shrugging my shoulders.

Lowering her voice, she said, "I'd started to worry a little."

"I understand."

"It's just me in the house after the kids go to bed, and . . . you know."

"Yeah, I can imagine," I said. "But everything's all right."

"Just let me know if you need anything," she said. Then she looked inside and gave me a quizzical look.

"West said he wanted to listen to some music."

"That's what that is?" she said with a slight smile.

"Yeah, that's the kind of stuff we like."

"Interesting," she said. "But really, though, if you need anything, don't hesitate to knock."

"Sure," I said. "Thanks a lot."

"Sorry for interrupting. It was rude of me, but I was just concerned."

"It's really okay. I was worried too."

"I tried to make this place nice for him," she said, lowering her voice again. "I know the bed isn't much, but I got him those curtains and the dish towels . . . "

"I'm sure he appreciates it," I said, holding my tongue about the baseboards.

"He seems like a nice guy," she said.

"Yeah, he's definitely a good one."

"Well, I'll let you two get back to talking."

"Thanks."

"Good night."

"Good night."

I closed the door – all the way this time – and walked slowly toward the bathroom. While passing in front of the window, I realized that anyone could see inside if they wanted to, so I unknotted the curtain and let it fall.

"Hey, I'm back," I said.

"Who was it?" he said.

"The landlord. She wanted to make sure everything was all right."

"She knows?"

"Well, I didn't have much of a choice," I said. "The gate was locked, and so was your front door."

"What's your opinion of her?"

"I mean, she seems nice," I said. "Pretty, too."

"I thought for a moment we might become involved."

"Really? I thought you'd sworn off all that."

"Don't worry, I came to my senses."

"Oh?"

"Yes. I need to get my own affairs in order before becoming involved."

"That's considerate," I said. "So are you ready to come out now?"

"Almost," he said. "But let me ask you, does anyone else know you're here?"

"No," I said. "My roommate thinks I went to the store."

"You should probably tell him what you're up to."

"That's a good idea." I took out my phone and typed, "I'm checking on West," and sent it. It took a while because my thumbs weren't behaving the way they should.

"And what about Melly? Does she know?"

"She's still at work," I said. "We're supposed to get together later."

"How is all of that going?" West said.

"Really well. I like her a lot."

"I feel a real kinship with her."

"Ah, that's great to hear, West," I said. "She's really fond of you too."

"Wonderful," said West. "Just one more thing for me, please."

"What's that?"

"Check under the pillow. I left you something."

"You didn't need to get me anything," I said. "I know you don't have any money."

"It felt important."

I went over to the bed, which was cluttered with West's notebooks and several medical bills. I lifted the pillow – it was one of my own pillows, he'd taken it without my knowing – and saw a book. "Aw, West. You shouldn't have."

"I know you haven't read that one yet," he said.

"That's right. You were just telling me about it the other night."

"There's a little inscription," he said. "Read it."

I leafed through the first few pages, then found it. "To M," it read. "Thanks for checking on me tonight. And thanks for helping me get situated in my new city – sorry I couldn't make it work. Your friend, West."

"Oh, West," I said, closing the book. "This is a really nice present."

"It was really nice of you to come," he said.

"It's no problem. I know you'd have done the same for me."

"Correct. We've always assisted each other."

"That's right."

"Do you mind turning the music up a bit more?"

"Sure, why?"

"I just feel as though it should be loud."

"Sure thing, West." I went back to the laptop and brought the sound up as high as it would go. The weird drone seemed to fill every corner of that dirty little house.

"Are you ready?" I said.

"Yes," he said. "Come closer."

"All right." I went and stood before the bathroom door. I could see my own shadow falling against it. "All set?"

"You know what you're going to find, don't you?"

"I have an idea."

"I used a scarf, though it didn't hurt as bad as you might think. I look terrible now, of course. Don't gaze at my face too long."

"I got it, West."

"At least there's no smell yet."

"Yeah, that's a good thing."

"Hopefully the kids will stay asleep."

"I hope so too, West."

"Ready?"

"Almost," I said. "I'd like to say one more thing, if that's all right."

"Of course."

"Just that I love you, very much, and that your friendship has been a gift and a real bright spot in my life."

"Thank you. I could say the same for you."

"Thanks, West."

"Anything else?"

"No," I said. "That's about it."

"Well then," he said. I opened the door.

OLD MOISTON

The air had a certain dampness to it that never seemed to leave, even in the coldest months, though it was rarely cold – Old Moiston also boasted nearly year-round heat . . .

After driving all night, we arrived in the middle of morning – it was a weekday, according to my phone. There was so little traffic and such a drowsy feeling in the streets that I wondered if the citizens were still sleeping. Sweetheart – who had slept peacefully the whole way – opened her eyes, then suggested we tour the different districts. I was happy to comply. First we drove uptown to see the grand mansions, then midtown to see the spreading trees, and finally downtown, through neighborhoods teeming with elegant, dilapidated buildings that seemed to me, in my sleep-deprived state, propped up by little more than damp hopes and wet dreams. While the energy capsules I'd ingested had gotten me through the drive, my mind was quickly becoming more and more submerged. Unable to push myself any further, I pulled into a shady spot, behind what looked to be a hearse. I mumbled something to Sweetheart, but my voice sounded funny, and soon I was drifting off . . .

I awoke some time later very confused. I was alone in the vehicle, and Sweetheart was nowhere to be seen, and the sheer number of people I now saw loitering on the sidewalks was cause for alarm. Suddenly, the door to a nearby house opened, and I saw some sort of ceremony happening inside. A dead man was stretched out on a cooling board, surrounded by candles and what looked to be loved ones. Tears were shed and prayers were murmured (I could tell by the way the mouths worked that deep things were being uttered), and then the body was placed in a coffin, and the mourners – Sweetheart shockingly among them – carried it out into the street and loaded it into the hearse. I was astounded by Sweetheart's empathy – not only was she crying the hardest and giving the hearse door the loudest pat with her hand once it closed, she was also the one clearly shouldering the most grief, letting those most affected take turns laying their heads against her neck.

Just then, a bumping band started up, and all the loiterers joined the loved ones and began dancing, Sweetheart too. After a while, I just couldn't take it anymore, watching Sweetheart dance so closely with all her new friends, so I crawled out of the sedan and joined the party. It took me a minute to get loose, but soon I was quite a presence on the block, and Sweetheart left her new friends and danced over to me. After grinding up and down my shaking frame while the others looked on in jealousy, she introduced me to her new friends, loved ones and loiterers alike, who were very genial and neighborly, and who assured me that everything was as it should be, that dancing in the streets so soon after a sad scene was strictly in accordance with city tradition. I must say I felt quite welcome: even if I suspected some around us had designs on Sweetheart or might be members of the criminal element, I didn't fail to be charmed by them as well as the great impromptu party they'd created – it was a proper introduction to the city for me and Sweetheart, and a fitting farewell for the dead man, who, I was informed, had been murdered at a similar party several days before. But there was no such trouble this time around: we kept the party going all night long, and before dawn broke, Sweetheart had, because of her new connections, arranged for us to take over the deceased's lease. All I had to do was put up the money and sign on the dotted line. The loved ones even graciously let me purchase the dead man's bed so we'd have a place to lay our heads.

We moved in that very morning, still buzzing. Our new residence was one half of an ancient house, with rooms in a straight line from front to back. Sweetheart and I crossed the threshold and locked the door behind us. We found ourselves in the living room, and I couldn't help but admire the previous occupant's pride in restoration and attention to detail. In fact, the preservation was so convincing that I half-expected to be greeted, upon entering, by a happy servant eager to please me. But it was the bedroom that was the most undeniably atmospheric: a curtained four-poster bed stood in the center of the room, illuminated by a red lantern that hung from the ceiling. I knew right away that we'd lucked out in acquiring the bed; not only was it a valuable antique, it also seemed designed to inspire maximum sexiness in whoever lay down in it.

We got in bed, Sweetheart and I, and kissed one another and spoke about the future. I asked her if she thought we would find what we were looking for here, and she said that she did, and I said I hoped so too. She asked me how my money was holding up and I told her fine, that I could afford not to work for a while, and I asked her about hers, and she said not good, so I told her she could depend on me for a little while. Then she asked me if I loved her, and I said I did, then wondered aloud why she would need to ask me such a question so soon after meeting me, and she said it was because she suffered from low self-esteem.

Given that I had just met and moved across the country with this person, this new information was worrisome to me, and potentially damaging to my own self-esteem, but I tried my best to put it out of my mind, and to do this more effectively, I reached out my hands and began fondling Sweetheart. Thankfully, she was interested in fondling me back. We also kissed for a long time, so long that I couldn't have said what time it actually was when we finished, so shut off from the world we were in that red room. And I really wanted to take things further, but just as I made the decisive move, she stopped me, pushing my hands away, and after kissing my lips very tenderly, and giving me one final fondle, she rolled over and said good night. It was hard for me not to proceed, but something gave me pause. I could see a slight shaking of her shoulders, and what sounded like quiet crying – tears of joy, I hoped, though I didn't inquire. They didn't last long, anyway, and soon, to my relief, she began to snore. I heard myself snoring too, right in time with her, so I rolled over – I cried a few tears then too, but they were tired tears, neither sad nor joyous, just water leaving my body. That's how we slept that night: backside to backside but soul to soul, on that curtained, sheetless, dead man's bed, far from home but not, I hoped, far from one another.

The following evening, after a particularly delicious dinner downtown, I asked Sweetheart to accompany me on a stroll along the banks of Old Moiston's largest waterway, the Moggy River, instead of heading directly to a nearby nightspot. She protested at first, citing a desire to find herself among her new friends as quickly as possible, but I spoke sweetly about the niceness of the night, about the link between strolling and digestion, and about how enjoyable it might be, for a change, to have a quiet conversation instead of shouting at each other over pulverizing music. She thought these were all fine reasons to take a stroll, but confessed that her desire for a cold refreshment might overpower her will to walk. I sympathized with this, so I suggested a compromise: if she would walk down to the Moggy with me, I promised that we could stop at a store along the way, purchase refreshments, and sip them as we strolled. She agreed, and we set off.

Down on the Moggy, a beautiful scene was unfolding. In the gathering dusk, young couples strolled together along the levee hand in hand. Sometimes they stopped to stretch, sometimes to study their surroundings; sometimes they leaned in to share a kiss.

There were others less active, but they were by no means lazy: some relaxed on the grass, under or over blankets, some strummed tunes on acoustic instruments, some smiled while sharing a light snack. Yet no matter what activity these couples were engaged in, their movements seemed so measured to me, so calmly and thoughtfully considered, that I found it impossible not to want to emulate them.

I took Sweetheart's hand and we joined the steady procession; all the pleasant, contented faces I saw assured me that we were welcome. On the water, barges sounded their low horns, and the wakes sent little waves sloshing against the bank. Rodents scurried to and fro along the river rocks, looking for morsels, while insects too small to see serenaded us with their sweet screeching. It's true that the path we walked was not well-lit, and the river was dark and deep nearby, but neither Sweetheart nor I felt even the slightest hint of danger. The atmosphere that night was close and convivial, and we'd been invited to join it.

I felt an overwhelming sense of relief. In fact, so much relief did I feel that I practically skipped for joy along the levee. If only Sweetheart shared my enthusiasm: at first, I noticed her devoting less pleasant attention to her surroundings, then her hand-holding pressure seemed to lessen, and finally she began talking to herself instead of me, and, based on her intonation, I could tell that her words weren't the kind the night seemed to invite. And then, as we passed a particularly happy couple staring silently into each other's eyes, Sweetheart wondered aloud in a dry, vacant voice if we had managed to die during dinner, and now found ourselves in the afterlife, walking amongst our fellow dead.

I told her that we had not died, so far as I knew, and that I didn't think it was fair to compare a pleasant stroll along the historic Moggy with the kind of bloodless trudge that some say awaits us on life's other side. After glancing down at her refreshment, I saw that the container was empty. I asked if she needed another, if maybe her lack of a fresh one was contributing to her testiness, but she sort of snarled at me and said that she hadn't reached that point in her life when her behavior was dictated by refreshments, thank you very much. Then, remembering the meal we'd just eaten, and Sweetheart's occasional intolerance for rich foods, I asked if perhaps her stomach was upsetting her, and making even an easy stroll difficult, but she replied – bitterly – that decadence had nothing to do with it: she loved the meal and hoped we would dine at the same establishment soon.

She said that what really bothered her about these people was that they were reminders of the kind of peaceful existence that had evaded her all her life. I told her that I understood, but still held out hope that if I found the right person, one suited to me both physically and mentally, one who raised my self-esteem while taking away my stress, then peace was possible, and the couples around us were living proof – each person around us had found the person most suited to them, even if it did cost them the kind of liveliness that was the hallmark of their earlier lives. Feeling moved by my own words, and buoyed by the sight of her beside me, I said that even though I'd only known her a short time, and been intimate with her for an even shorter one, I believed that she could be that person to me, a life partner and a partner for life, one that never stopped calming and comforting me, who would stay by my side wherever I wandered, whether I found myself by the Moggy or by some river far away.

Stunned, she gazed into my eyes, and, failing to see all the love that was in them, angrily shook her head, then sat down on the edge of the bank, her legs dangling over the water. I tried to hug and comfort her, but she swatted my arms away, telling me to leave her in peace. I tried again, this time on the other side, but her response was the same, only more forceful. Rather than let the situation escalate, I decided to give Sweetheart her space: I wandered over to a nearby bench and sat down next to a napping friend, who, in his hurry to fall asleep, had forgotten to finish his refreshment. While helping myself to it, I made certain not to let Sweetheart out of my sight.

But she made no sudden moves. In fact, as I watched her in between the strolling couples, I couldn't help but notice what a helpless, forlorn figure she cut there on the ground. It occurred to me that she might have been younger than I'd thought; she certainly looked rather childlike, shivering and clutching herself. She suddenly became aware of being watched – she spotted me and shooed me away again. I didn't have to be told twice, not this time. I got up from the bench and joined the couples, and with them I strolled the length of the riverwalk. It was a good bit lonelier this time, but I pretended that Sweetheart's absence didn't bother me: I kept my eyes focused on the beautiful surroundings, politely acknowledged my fellow strollers, stopped to stretch when I thought my muscles would most appreciate it. I even introduced myself to some of the couples, telling them my story and situation, how I had recently moved to Old Moiston with Sweetheart and how I hoped to make friends I could be comfortable around, and while they listened sensitively to me, it was clear that, without Sweetheart by my side, they had trouble seeing me as anything but a loiterer, or worse, a criminal – someone who desired their ears only so he could more easily get their wallet. Sometimes they even failed to register my presence.

When I reached the walkway's end, where the concrete gave way to the famous Moggy mud, I stood for a long time against the railing, gazing out on the river and reflecting on the situation. My rejection by the river people was less a blow than I expected. Many of them seemed, though well-meaning, rather boring, and, beyond their ease of being, perhaps there really wasn't much else to them. But one thing was clear to me at that moment: Sweetheart was the only being who mattered to me, and I vowed then and there – to myself, to the Moggy, and to anyone that would hear – that I would do whatever it took to keep her front and center in my life.

Just then I felt a vibration in my pocket, and, fishing out my phone, I saw that Sweetheart was calling. I smiled, knowing that she'd come to her senses. But rather than answer I just let it ring, teasing her a little, and began strolling back toward her, weaving in and out of the couples that stood in my way. If she still sat facing the Moggy all the better, I thought, because I'd be able to surprise her, throw my arms around her and show her just how much she meant to me. But when I reached the spot where she had recently sat, she was nowhere to be found – instead, a small crowd had gathered.

Out of breath, I sat myself down and called Sweetheart. Getting her greeting instead of her live voice, I tried again, but with the same result. I checked my own mailbox, but there were no messages. I then became more aware of my surroundings and could hear many of the couples crying out, could see their eyes nervously scanning the Moggy. I rose from my seat and joined the onlookers, still calling Sweetheart. I fought through the crowd to see what they all gazed at: far out in the middle of the Moggy, I could faintly make out a waving hand. My heart dropped. I called her phone again, praying she would pick up, safe and far away, but again it was only her spacey greeting: *I am away, I am away, I am away. Leave something for me, for I am away.*

I asked the onlookers what the swimmer looked like, but none could come up with a consistent picture. The gender was unclear, the hair length too. The age was also a mystery: no one saw the swimmer go in. I looked harder at the hand. It was impossible to tell the kind of person it belonged to. To compound the problem, the evening had grown foggy, and little wisps hovered around the appendage. Yet I knew I had to act – I remembered the vow I had just made and intended to see it through. I kicked off my shoes and stripped off my suit, got all the way down to my underclothes, and the onlookers cleared a path for me to the edge of the bank. I left my phone with a trustworthy onlooker, carefully instructing him how to use it in case Sweetheart called, and what to say: *I am away – I am away, Sweetheart, I am away. But I'll return – I'll return – I'll return someday.*

I stepped down onto the slimy rocks. I waded in, first to my ankles, then to my knees, and finally to my waist. The water was cold and smelled of old trash. Through the fog, I spied the hand. I dove in and started swimming. Immediately I felt myself carried sideways, so I fought hard against the current, angling myself in such a way that I might get close. But after a particularly hard push, I opened my eyes and saw that the hand was now far off to my right. I looked to the bank, and, seeing the crowds, was able to orient myself. I recalibrated and tried again, taking an even wider angle this time, arcing against the current so I'd be certain to hit my mark, but when I next opened my eyes I saw it was now off to my left.

I decided to head straight for it. Ignoring the dark, spongy shapes sucking at me, I put my head down and kicked with all my might, and when next I opened my eyes, I was very close. The hand was stuck in an eddy, swirling round and round amongst some pieces of trash. Without fear I entered the vortex, letting myself be swirled sideways. For a moment the hand and I occupied opposite poles, swirling equidistant from each other, neither coming closer nor growing apart, locked in a dance as old as time itself, but then the hand began to droop considerably, and I knew it was time to cross the divide: I reached out and attained it, grasping it with my own just as it started its descent. Working down the arm, the shoulder, and finally to the skull, I pulled it out of the water, and in the hazy light I peered into its face. For a moment I thought that the face was my father's, but that was wishful thinking: the face was my face; I seemed, for an instant, to be holding my own head. The long lashes, the large lips – it was my face, only paler, more serene, a face whose concerns were no longer of this world.

Of course it wasn't me. Though close to death myself, I hadn't lost my sense of reality. The head belonged to another young man, just another lost young man in a world full of lost young men. Perhaps he was a local, perhaps a tourist. Perhaps he drowned saving his Sweetheart; perhaps he had confessed his love and been rejected, and in his sorrow gone for a fatal swim. Perhaps the answer was simpler: he'd had too many refreshments that night, taken leave of his clothes, his senses, and his faculties, and I now held the sad results. But whatever decision had guided him into my arms that night, the sight of my pale brother now touched me deeply – I brought his face to mine and kissed his pale cheek. *Be at peace*, I thought.

But the current was cruel: it ripped the two of us from the safety of the eddy and rushed us swiftly downstream. I held to him with all my might, and we swirled and spiraled together. River water filled my mouth, and it seemed that death was close. Only moments before, when I had discovered that the hand belonged to someone else, I'd been relieved – I knew I'd get to see my love again. But now, realizing that the Moggy was going to claim me, I felt something stranger: I wished that Sweetheart really had drowned, that she had gone for a swim and been taken under. I pictured her sleeping soundly at the bottom of the river, waiting for me. I vowed that when I too was taken and dragged down, that I would, even after death, summon the strength to crawl along the bottom, back upriver, and lay by her side. And there we would lie, Sweetheart and I, awaiting the day when our skins would loosen and slide away and our bones would lightly land upon each other's.

But just as my strength and hope was fading, and I had issued my final prayer – *please please please spare me, wonderful God* – the current suddenly gave us up, and the river grew wonderfully calm. The young man, now floating face down, seemed to offer himself, and I gratefully draped my body across him. He made for a fine, if unconventional, raft. I took a few deep breaths, and once I was fully relaxed, instead of heading straight for shore, I decided to simply let the current carry me for a while, not worrying where I was bound. I was exhausted, sure, and still in doubt as to what had become of Sweetheart, but I felt cut free in a way that made me a little giddy. I soon found myself floating peacefully in the middle of the wide river, and was compelled to look around.

It's incredible what you encounter along a river at night, the secret places you're given access to. The first sight I was treated to was a factory, where such intense work was taking place that flames shot up from two of its tallest columns. And while I could not see what they were busy making, I was certain something significant was afoot – the sounds of metal on metal reached me even in the middle of the river. Next I spied a building deep in darkness, and had the fog not momentarily broken I'm sure I would have missed it – there was not a single light on its exterior, yet I could feel the rumblings and vibrations as I passed it. None of this would be worth noting except that, floating by this mysterious building, the water I rafted in went from merely dirty to downright filthy – I had to plug all my holes just to be able to endure it. I then passed a large compound, fenced in by high wire and lit so brightly I was certain it was a sports stadium. But then I heard sorrowful songs on the breeze and understood it was a penal institution. Moved by those strong, simple melodies, I turned my thoughts to all those behind bars throughout the world, all those souls forgotten by society, too dangerous to roam free, perhaps, but not without a degree of dignity either – and I blessed them. I blessed myself as well, and Sweetheart – I was in a wonderfully forgiving mood.

Soon I felt the mud rise up under my feet, and I was thankful for it – no doubt, in my meditative state, I might have followed the river clear down to the mouth, then out to sea – *then what would have become of me?* I stood up on the shoal, stretched, and sent the raft downstream. I climbed the bank and entered the woods, my clothes still dripping. The moon shone through just enough for me to navigate, and I blazed a soggy trail back toward town.

All's well that ends wet in Old Moiston, after all . . .

THE NIGHT YOU DIED

The night you died, Japh and I were supposed to attend a going-away party. Not yours, someone else's, an acquaintance you were not fond of. We were about to leave for the party when I suddenly said to Japh, "We should probably go check on him. I haven't heard from him in three days and I'm getting worried," to which Japh replied, "That's probably the right thing to do."

We drove the Volvo, the same car you had used to move your possessions there a few weeks before. Later my coworker, your landlord, whose house you defiled the night you died, would refer to the Volvo as The Doom Wagon.

To avoid any unnecessary drama, in case nothing was actually the matter the night you died, Japh and I used the pretext of the going-away party to gain access to the side gate, which led to your apartment. "He was supposed to come with us to a going-away party," we said to your landlord, my coworker, as she stood in her doorway, "but he's not answering his phone."

This lie was quickly exposed when, after she unlocked the gate, and Japh and I walked around back, saw your lights on, knocked repeatedly at your door, and found it locked, we returned to the front of the house and were forced to explain why it was imperative that we be let into your apartment.

It was your landlord's husband who let us in. If he was at all fond of me before the night you died, he was understandably less so

111

after. According to another coworker, he resented my failure to mention your history of depression and suicidal ideations when recommending you for the apartment.

As we stood outside your bathroom door, Japh and I gripped each other and attempted to prepare for the coming horror. "Let's be strong," we said, unfortunately resorting to cliché. "Are you ready? Yes, I'm ready. Okay, let's do this."

I'm certain you didn't anticipate this the night you died, but as soon as I turned the handle, your body, which was pressed against the door somehow, tumbled out. I jumped back and screamed; Japh jumped back and screamed too. The landlord's husband, who was behind us, also jumped back, but instead of screaming he groaned.

The night you died, while you lay on the cold floor, I caught a glimpse of your face. Your eyes were suspicious, accusatory, half-closed, your mouth a slightly sardonic frown. It was a familiar look, a face you made often. But this time, as Japh noted, "It was wrong."

Several police cars arrived the night you died, lights flashing but without sirens. The lights would continue flashing, without stopping, for the next few hours, only heightening the lurid, carnivalesque feel of the proceedings.

We led the police to the back of the house the night you died, detailing exactly how we had come to find you. We pointed to where your body could be found, but did not, for the sake of our own mental health, enter with them.

The night you died, it was decided that I would call your father – I seem to recall, in a moment of ill-conceived bravery, volunteering. I scanned my contacts but didn't see his name. I reported this to Japh, who thought Mil might have it, so he walked to the corner to call him. When he returned, he reported that Mil said he did not have it, but Mil knew that Gehn would, and he had taken it upon himself to call her. Soon I received a message from Mil with your father's number.

Your father picked up immediately the night you died. "Mr. Smith, I have some terrible news," I began, and then told him, as gently as I could, what happened. After regaining composure, he asked what method you had used, and I told him. He asked if you had left a note, and I said I hadn't looked. He then asked that I send him your phone, your computer, your notebooks, the note if there was one, and any other objects we thought he might want.

Your landlord, my coworker, brought Japh and me mugs of hot mint tea the night you died. We drank our hot mint tea and shivered. "Just to be clear," she said, "were you really on your way to a going-away party?"

The night you died, a detective, who had the face of a leopard, said he wanted to speak to me. I assented, and he suggested that we talk in his car, where it was warm. He wanted to know how long I had known you, and my understanding of your mental health. I told him everything, was completely honest, but when he inquired about your drug use history, so as not to implicate myself, I said you had none.

The detective was also a bit confused as to your line of work and asked if you were a nurse. The scrubs you were wearing the night you died confused him. I explained that those were just your house

113

clothes, that you wore scrubs by choice, that you found them comfortable, that you were a waiter by trade, like me.

When they wheeled you out in a bag the night you died, Japh and I were caught unprepared and only managed a meek goodbye. "Goodbye," we said softly, as they trundled you past. "Goodbye."

The night you died, the coroner's investigator, who had the face of a hectored sitcom father, asked Japh and me to accompany him back to your death room. Once inside, he asked that we re-enact the scene of us entering and finding you, which we begrudgingly did. "We walked in like this," I said, going out and walking back in. "And when we got to the door, I turned the handle and he came tumbling out."

"The thing I can't figure out," said the coroner's investigator, "is what he hung himself from. He was on the floor when we found him – he wasn't hanging from anything." "It does seem like there are abrasions in the wood here at the top," Japh said, examining the door. "I'm no expert, but he might have knotted one end of the sheet, thrown it over the door, and closed it." But the coroner's investigator remained unconvinced. "Here's what I'd like you to do," he said. "Stay out of here until the autopsy results come back."

The night you died, Japh and I had an impromptu gathering at our house. Kelzey came, as did Wim, Scote, Morg, Jin, and Larsen. Perhaps there were others. We sat in a circle in my bedroom, and no one spoke. We passed a bottle around, around and around.

Later on, I received a call from the coroner's investigator and excused myself from the circle. He had a few more questions for me – what medications you had been on, for exactly how long you had been depressed – and seemed highly suspicious of my answers.

I drunkenly biked over to Kelzey's very late the night you died, in need of a warm body. After talking, we made quick, extremely intense love in her bed. As soon as I closed my eyes to sleep, I had a vision of your face. Your eyes were open, you were smiling, but then you started hissing and I realized that you were trying to swallow me down into Hell.

Other Thoughts:
For several days after the night you died, I spent hours at the computer, attempting to write a story that dramatized the night you died. I cast myself as the protagonist, I eliminated Japh entirely. Its centerpiece was a hallucinated conversation between my character and yours. Those familiar with the situation found it a moving, if morbid, tribute, and those who weren't found it utterly baffling.

When Ghen and Mil came down the week after the night you died, they wanted to see the house. I walked them toward it, but right around the corner from it, I grew weak and couldn't go any farther. They were very understanding and asked me to describe what it looked like, which I did to the best of my ability. Soon after, they met me in a nearby park. They showed me a picture they had taken of your house. It was the wrong house.

A full year later, while in the midst of a psilocybin trip, on a farm quite far from where you died, I detected a whirring sound coming from deep inside the house, which caused my knees to buckle and my head to swim. It was a fan – someone had left a fan on in a bathroom deep inside the house, just as you had done the night you died.

Last Thoughts:
I couldn't open doors without fear for many months after the night you died.

It's a regret of mine that I didn't embrace you the night you died. The night you died was not the actual night you died. The autopsy placed your time of death in the early morning, two days prior. I hope you'll forgive the cheap gimmick of the refrain; "the night you died to me" didn't quite have the same ring.

I've been wearing your boots, which I found while cleaning out your apartment, for several years now. When I leave town for good this summer, I will finally, if I am strong enough, throw them out.

I truly hope that I am not still thinking about the night you died on the night I die. That, it seems to me, would be a waste of precious time.

Postscript:
Much of this was composed at the coffee shop where we used to meet, at the same outside table where we used to sit, where the breeze would blow your beautiful unkempt hair around, and where you communicated, a few weeks before the night you died, that every day was a struggle for you, that death reared its head to you every morning – afternoon – evening without fail, and that my hope for you – you were only 34, brilliant, wonderful – was greatly misplaced.

MICKEY'S PRAYER

Mickey was praying one evening, alone in his bedroom. Summer was over . . . so much had happened, yet he hadn't even prayed once. Now he was naked to the waist on his carpeted floor, in child's pose: his forehead pressed to the carpet, his eyes closed. An ambient LP – Mickey was quite the collector – was on the turntable, playing at low volume. His laptop was in the living room where he'd deliberately left it . . .

The first person he prayed for was his brother Maddy, who lived in California. "I hope his eBay business succeeds," he prayed, "and I hope the chickens in the coop he built survive." He also prayed that Maddy would stand up for himself more often: "There's no reason he should pay a third of the power bill when there's five people living in that house. And his boss should give him more time off."

Then his thoughts turned to his mother. He saw her lying on a white sofa, also in California, watching one of her crime shows. "I hope she's doing well," he prayed. "She'll be ten years cancer-free in November, and that's a great accomplishment. But I worry about those shows she watches. Every night before bed she gorges on violence and tidy police work, and that can't be good for her mind. Sure, she's got the book club, and she's got Dad, but I hope she finds the strength to stay away from those shows."

"Of course Dad's in my prayers as well," Mickey continued, "and here's hoping his caseload increases – God knows he needs to keep working so he has something to do. And sister Ebby, she's in my thoughts. She's always so busy, keeping that nonprofit afloat."

"I wish they weren't all so far away," Mickey thought, shifting his position slightly. "It was a hell of a thing I did, moving to the other side of the country. And for what? I don't regret it, but sometimes I think I should have stayed put. It's pretty in California, and I probably could have found a job teaching high school or something. I should visit them over the holidays, or at least video chat them soon. It's always good to see their faces . . . "

Mickey sighed and tried to gauge how much time was left on the LP's side. "Probably another few minutes or so," he thought. "Well, that's all right. There are plenty of others I could pray for tonight, people more in my day-to-day orbit. They'd probably be embarrassed to learn that I was praying for them, but that's okay – they don't have to know."

The first person Mickey thought about was his friend Jelby. He saw her posing in her pink bedroom, taking nude photos of herself. "Yeah, Jelby is definitely someone I should pray for," he thought. "I hope she finds some peace in her life, particularly with regards to her looks – I hope she doesn't get any more tattoos. I like some of them, but the last few have been really trashy and show poor judgment. She's got great style, but soon she's not going to have any natural skin left, and that'll be a shame."

"Colum could definitely benefit from some prayer too," Mickey thought, picturing his friend smoking on a seedy street corner. "Oh yeah, definitely. The last time we got together, he told me he'd started sleeping with strangers for money. He claims it's for an art project, but if you ask me, he's courting disaster."

Just then Mickey heard pots and pans clanging in the kitchen, and he realized that his roommate Rafe was throwing together some food. "I hesitate to do this with him so close," Mickey thought, "but I want to pray for Rafe – he could use a little luck. He's been working so hard on his music lately, but it doesn't seem to be paying off in the fan department. I pray he finds success soon, or takes up something more conventional."

"And as for me," he quickly added, "I guess I pray I spend less time on my laptop, and maybe take up gardening. I think I need to stop drinking, but easier said than done. But all in all, things are pretty good. Fall will be here soon, and I'm already thinking about what I'll be for Halloween . . . "

The LP abruptly reached the end of the side. The needle lifted, and immediately all the ambience in the room was gone. "Well, that felt good to do," Mickey blurted out, opening his eyes.

MY WORST IDEAS 2

I.

A mother's son goes away to war, and when he comes back, he comes back very changed. She can't quite figure out what's going on with him, but he's noticeably different. Maybe it's in the eyes or maybe it's in the smile or in the hands, but at any rate something is going on with him. And she's trying hard to figure out what it is, asking him all sorts of questions about how it was over there and what he ate, although the son's not giving her much to go on. He's really vague about everything, maybe even elusive, but he assures her over and over again that he was just following his orders and that he behaved like the kind of person she raised him to be. The mother is satisfied, more or less, until one day she decides to go snooping around his room and she finds his wallet, and in the wallet there is a picture of this young boy she has never seen before – he is clearly foreign. Her son is taking a bath while all this is going on and has no idea that his mother is snooping through his wallet. So he gets out and dries off and comes back to his bedroom and sees that his mother has laid out the young boy's picture on his pillow, and he picks it up and stares at it and anger flashes across his face, but then he calmly returns it to his wallet and gets dressed. Downstairs, he meets his mother, who is eating eggs, and she offers some to him, but he pours himself cold cereal instead, and while they're eating at the table she confronts him about the photo, and he tells her it's none of her business, will never be any of her business; she says that because he's just come home and can't yet make it on his own and has to live under her roof that his business is automatically her business, and then the son pulls a knife on his mother, but then puts it away and says that he didn't mean it. The mother represses this and goes about her day, and for a few hours it seems that everything will be fine. But around dinnertime something small happens and they get into it again, and again the knife is pulled and it seems that he really will stab her this time, but just before he can, his father comes home from work and wrestles it from his son's hands. All three of them stand around facing each other, breathing heavily. Then we will move back in time: the young boy from the photo is seen, trapped in a burning room and crying out for help, and the son is seen trying to break down the door to save him. He is unable to, and the boy burns. Then we will come back to the present and see all three family members embracing.

II.

A brother is having a hard time convincing his younger brother to stop using drugs, and he is ready to take drastic measures. He is simply at the end of his rope, and he's tried just about every trick in the book. But then an idea hits him, and he makes some arrangements and flies to the place where the brother is living, drags him single-handedly out of his drug den, and drives him to a national forest, which is maybe an hour from the city. They don't speak on the way to the forest, but that is partially because the older brother has carefully selected a soundtrack, which he plays for the younger brother while they drive. The songs are mostly sentimental songs that the brothers used to enjoy together, that they used to sing to one another when they were little, but at the end of the mix a song comes up, one that the younger, drug-addled brother doesn't recognize, and with a grin on his face the older brother admits that he wrote this song special for the occasion. The younger brother is impressed: he didn't really think his older brother was capable of such beauty and depth. But this song, and we experience it start to finish with the brothers, is really just a red herring. At the trailhead, the older brother tells his younger brother to get out of the car and walk, which the younger one does, although with a suspicious look on his face, and then the two brothers walk along a winding path for a while, and not much is heard except for the older brother's humming, humming that song he wrote to commemorate the occasion. What the older brother can't see as he walks behind his younger brother is that the younger brother is continuing to ingest drugs as he walks – he is bringing them up from his jacket pocket and swallowing them without water. The younger brother is simply becoming more and more insane with every step. A little while later they reach a clearing, and the younger brother asks him what he has planned, and the older brother must admit that he really doesn't have a plan – he just wanted to go on a walk with his younger brother and spend time with him and see if he could convince him to stop abusing drugs, at which point the younger brother pulls a knife on his older brother. A struggle ensues, and the older brother, who is sober and in good shape, disarms and kills his younger brother. We see blood on the leaves. He stands over the body and cries for a while before he calls his sister, who has been sober three years, and tells her what happened. After that, we move forward in time, and we meet the older brother on a speaking tour. He isn't talking about drugs, but some other subject. He is hollow-looking and exhausted and in need of a friend. After one of his speeches, he meets a woman he likes, and they have dinner later that night. At dinner the older brother spills his guts about what happened with his younger brother and admits that he is probably incapable of being a good romantic partner. But the woman says she believes in second chances and non-traditional relationships and that's where we leave them, both at the dinner table, smiling at one another.

III.

A prisoner is awaiting execution and is trying to decide what his last meal will be. There are several people in his cell with him – a priest, his mother, and his favorite teacher. Everyone is encouraging him to choose the rare steak, but the prisoner wants something more humble, the chicken with a slice of pie, something nice and basic to digest slowly in his last moments. But the priest is adamant that he pick the rare steak, and he communicates this to the prisoner with his eyes, by lifting his eyebrows, and he's not the only one – the prisoner's mother and the teacher send messages with their eyes that they are in agreement that he should choose the rare steak. So the prisoner realizes something is up and agrees to order the steak, and the priest calls the prison guard over, who has been patiently waiting down the hall, and he gives the meal request to the guard, and the guard writes it down in a notepad and nods his head and walks away, and we stay with the guard and are privy to his thoughts while he walks the length of the labyrinthine prison, all the way to the kitchen. He thinks about his wife and children back home, and how much he's looking forward to seeing them after his long miserable shift is over. He says hello to the chef and puts in the prisoner's order, and then we watch the chef study the order and nod and begin preparing the meal, at which point we return to the prisoner and the priest and the mother and the teacher in the cell, and we hear them make small talk, but even these banal exchanges are interesting and fraught with deeper meaning because of what we know the priest and the others did with their brows. Although they are talking about the weather, it soon becomes clear they are hatching an escape plan – the priest, having sat in on so many state murders, knows for a fact that they will serve the rare steak with a sharp knife, which the priest will pocket after the meal is complete. And when the guard asks for it, the prisoner will say he doesn't know what happened to it, and they will search the prisoner and every nook and cranny of the teacher and maybe the mother but more than likely not the priest, because

124

he is trusted. Just before the injection is administered, the priest will pretend to have something to say to the executioner, but instead of saying it he will actually let the knife fall from his sleeve into his hand and cut the executioner's throat, and when the guard and the warden reach for their guns the mother and teacher will hold their arms fast behind them, and the priest will turn and cut their throats too. It will be like a dance he makes around the room, cutting throats, even the throats of the victims' families – he plans to spare no one. However, just as our chef is passing the steak dinner out of the kitchen, the warden appears, and on a whim, he decides to inspect the dish. He notices the knife, how remarkably sharp it is, and, suddenly sensing what the priest has planned, slips it into his pocket. In the very next scene we see him in the cell, standing over the four conspirators – the condemned man, the priest, the mother, and the teacher – forcing them to eat the rare steak with their hands, while the guard covers his eyes nearby.

THE RIDDLER

A blessed evening to ye, brother. Where might ye be these days?

I'm in North Henderson.

And how are things progressing?

Things could be better.

A feeling I'm most familiar with. What do you lack?

I could have more work. More friends.

Friends will always find ye, dear brother, if they know which rock to look under. And you can always sell thyself.

I'm in an apartment with Mitt. It's near the cemetery and the fairgrounds.

You paint a perfect picture I long to hang on my wall.

Are you still in the shack?

I'm still in the shit shack, where I will always and forever be.

It's snowing here.

It never snows here, brother.

The other night, I hiked three miles in the snow for a blowjob.

How fared the blower?

He wouldn't turn off the movie he'd been watching.

Was it a porno? Mayhap he needed coaching.

It was about a tuba player who suffered from schizophrenia.

My, my, how that tickles my funny bone. How's thy mental health?

I'm really glad I got out of the South.

Hard to rest easy in the belly o' the beast.

I couldn't take a walk without being reminded of some fatality.

But now North Henderson opens up its frigid arms to ye. And with frosty lips it welcomes ye.

My room isn't much to look at, though.

So ye found ye a little shit shack of your own, have ye?

Mitt gave me a choice. He said, "One of the rooms is very big and faces the street and the other is small and coffin-shaped and in the back. What'll it be?"

And the generous soul I know ye to be said, "The back's enough for me."

Do you think I suffer intentionally?

It afflicteth our whole family.

I was thinking of Mitt. And also money.

You were, were ye?

Mitt just went through a divorce. I thought he might benefit from a less shitty room.

And money?

The back's a hundred dollars cheaper.

Thou wert protecting thine assets, then. Our father would be beaming.

I sold almost everything before moving.

Better sold than stolen, mine brother.

I can't believe they repo'd your car.

If only I'd been a good borrower and not defaulted.

Did they ever find the drugs?

Methinks they wound up on the street.

And Del, is he still hanging around?

Del-son? Where else would the poor childe go?

Why do you call him Del-son?

Because he is like a son to me. Is that so odd?

Maybe, given what his parents did to him. Isn't he your age?

Still, I must regard him as a son.

He really made me mad a few months back.

Oh?

You and I were talking – don't you remember? He butted in and said I shouldn't say those things to you.

Aye, he's quite protective. But it was a touchy subject ye had brought up.

I still think you should get sober.

Are we going to beat this mutilated horse again, brother?

No. Are you still seeing Valea?

Aye, it is a blessed union.

That's great. I remember last time you were waffling.

Last time I was speculating that she might be too mad even for me.

Is she still having episodes?

She is a seer of strange visions, brother. But I have come to love them. And she bringeth a winsome energy to the shit shack.

Do you ever hear from Adley?

Now and then, although she knows I'm spoken for.

Does she still have that channel?

Wherein she describes in detail the alien being that impregnated her, and the beautiful children she bore him? Aye.

You were a big believer in that stuff a few years ago.

I won't deny an abiding interest in our extraterrestrial brethren.

I still remember that conversation in the hot tub.

Ye argued passionately against the existence of lizard people, and she for.

One of the weirdest nights of my life.

How green ye still are, brother. But enough of lizards and love: tell me more about your abode.

There's a legless brown couch in the living room. In the kitchen there's the biggest butcher block I've ever seen. There's a small closet in my bedroom – the last tenant left a back scratcher on the rack.

Oh, my my my, there goes my funny bone again. I must say that for a man in a shit shack, this sounds quite dreamy.

Dreamy, yeah.

Are you still seeing Stan's face before ye fall asleep?

Sometimes. I'm not far from where he's buried.

I thought the poor soul was cremated down south.

He was, but his family had the ashes sent up here.

Brother, is this the real reason you moved to North Henderson?

No. I hope not. Really I just came here to hang out with Mitt and do some writing.

And what is flowing from thy golden pen in North Henderson?

I started a story about clowns the other day.

A most prescient subject this day and age.

I can't seem to write anything good anymore.

Be that as it may, it often bringeth me great pride to think of My Brother The Writer. I myself long for a sturdier identity.

It's garbage, that stuff.

Do you remember that celebration we threw for our dear mother, on the occasion of her 60th?

Of course. You sang "Lay, Lady, Lay" while out of your mind.

But something else happened that day, a very sad thing for me.

I think I know what it is.

Our mother's friend Wennie cornered us. "It's Marty," she said. "The Writer! And Ellie, The Doctor!" But when she came to me, she couldn't think of anything to say – her mouth hung open.

I said you were The Riddler.

And I loved thee more that day than any other. But of course you were just smoothing things over. The Great Writer is also The Great Mediator.

Have you been in touch with Ellie?

We went for a kindly stroll some months ago. I was not at my most droll.

She mentioned you seemed upset.

I came with the intention of strengthening the bond, and she didn't want to speak of anything substantial.

She said she liked seeing your face.

It is a nice visage, isn't it?

Yes.

Methinks it has only improved with pain.

You've got thick hair too.

Would that it were true for both of us, brother.

Yeah, mine's going fast.

And what of our mother and father? What sweet breezes blow from home?

Nothing good. Dad's still worried about his lack of clients.

And our mother?

She got mugged the other day outside of exercise class, but she's okay.

I confess that there were times I was tempted to lift some of her jewelry.

Really?

Methought: she doesn't need all of it! But when I went looking in the drawer, it was gone.

I'm glad you don't live with them anymore.

Aye, a cursed arrangement.

They kept your room the same, you know?

May it remain a spectral space.

It's there if you need it.

Did ye know that I camped on the hill above the house for a spell? This was before I found the shit shack, of course.

I didn't know.

I don't hold it against ye, brother. Ye were far away, and had plenty of problems of thine own.

I would have helped get you a hotel.

I know, brother. You never begrudged me a little gold when the gales were blowing.

How was it up there? On the hill?

I didn't sleep a wink, brother. Might ye guess why?

No.

Coyotes, brother. They prowled around all night, yipping and howling. Paco Dog was tearing his larynx in fright.

It's like that story you used to tell when you were little. About Big Brother.

Big Brother, yes. He who was not you, but looked like you, and who, unlike you, had super powers.

It took place on a hill, didn't it?

Aye. Big Brother brought me to a hill with many coyotes. The coyotes attacked, and Big Brother shot them all. One almost bit my leg off!

I was always jealous of your imagination.

And I was jealous of thine ease in the world.

Well, that's changed now.

Aye, you've gotten a bit mauled. It makes me love you all the stronger.

Thanks, brother. How's Paco Dog?

He's at my feet right now. Smelling malodorous.

I miss that guy.

Tell me something, brother. Is it thy preference to be buried or cremated? I have been musing on this matter as of late.

Cremated, I suppose. You?

I used to feel cremation was the way. But the texts I've been devouring lately suggest that a body be allowed to putrefy, so alchemy might occur.

I'm familiar with the process.

Aye, a writer loves his alchemy. Will ye be so kind as to write me a story one day?

Of course. Anything in particular you'd like it to include?

My jingle-jangle voice, my queer way with words. My general philosophy.

And what is that, exactly?

Society grinds the good ones to dust, while the villains enjoy equanimity.

Sure, sounds about right.

I suspect ye would know what to call it.

Of course.

And ye would hold nothing back, would ye? No sugarcoating?

No sugarcoating.

Dead men need no sugarcoating, brother. The living need it even less.

But a little sugar is nice sometimes. Do you need money?

Brother, you know The Riddler doesn't need money. He liveth on riddles alone.

Do you?

Mayhap I might put fifty American dollars to good use, if ye can spare them.

Sure, I'll do it right now.

Thank ye, my good brother. I wish ye great luck on thy clown story.

Thanks, I'll need it.

And remember: if thy life continues to slide, ye always have a patch here at the shit shack.

Be careful what you wish for, brother.

Be careful what you wish for, brother.

Goodbye for now.

Goodbye, brother.

Born in the Bay Area of California, Michael Jeffrey Lee spent time in New Orleans and now lives in Berlin. Sarabande Books published his first short story collection, *Something in My Eye*, in 2012. Lee's stories have appeared in *N+1*, *The Rupture*, and *BOMB*, among many others. He received the Mary McCarthy Prize in Short Fiction and a literary grant from the Berlin Senate. In addition, he is the vocalist for Budokan Boys and teaches writing at The Reader Berlin.